# When Souls Touch
# Letters From A Caged Heart

LaShawn McCallum

Soul Heart Publishing

Copyright © 2020 by LaShawn McCallum

Book Cover Design by Michael Corvin

ISBN: 978-0-578-79115-9 (paperback)

*This book is dedicated to the one who always loved me unconditionally. My life was never complete without you. You showed me the real true definition of what a man looks like. You loved me flaws and all, even when I couldn't see the beauty in myself. You always been and will continue to be my protector. This love I have for you will never die out even when we leave this Earth. Modern day Ossie and Ruby love.*
*Love is Love.... Thank You Pooh Bear.*

# Introduction: LaShanna's Thoughts

Damn really after all these years our relationship has turned into one of these situations. I never wanted to be that typical girl from the hood always doing something like this when it comes to a guy. But you were not just another guy to me that I could turn my back on. My heart would not just rest without me knowing if you were okay. You were my childhood friend that always was there when I needed you since the sixth grade. I remember I could not wait to get home, so I can talk to you on the phone. I remember your ass would be on punishment and you sneaking to use the phone before your mother got home. Shit you really did not care if you got caught and it could have added more time on to your punishment. Now we are two fucking grown ass adults in our 20's and it feels like we are still in the sixth grade again. This time around its different for us because you are not free and doing time for something that you were not involved in. My mind cannot wrap around the fact you are in prison and you should not be in that fucked up place is killing me inside. I would be breaking my number one rule that I said I would never do, but never say never cause now I am that typical girl from the hood writing to a man in prison. Fuck it I will write you cause at the end of the day I will always be around to make sure you are okay just like you would do the same for me. This relationship is unbreakable, and nothing could stand in its way not even ten years of prison, or could it?

Sentence Starts Now...
Let's Begin Caged Heart Journey

2-14-2010

Happy V Day

LaShanna,

I am trying to relax myself because I do not want to overwhelm you with all the things I am feeling right now. It is very good to hear from you, sweetheart. There were so many times that I wanted to call you, but I could not find the words to say. I wrote you over the summertime on your birthday, then once again in October, and when you did not respond, I figured that you moved on with your life and wasn't beat. I smiled the whole way through reading your letter because I never thought I would speak to you again. I am proud of you for following through and graduating college. Since you went, then I don't have to. I also miss our conversations and experiences we shared in each other's life. I can't believe that I am writing you from here, I never saw this coming. To answer your question, remember back in 2006 when I was arrested because so called friends of mine picked me up in a stolen car? Well as a result, I was sentenced to eight years. Two of which I completed last week. I am holding it together as best I can, but I would give anything for my situation to be different. So many others have come in and out of my life since I been away, so I want you to know ahead of time that I really appreciate the fact that you did write me. In case we lose contact again for whatever reason, please remember that you are deeply loved now as you were back then. And wherever life takes us, my love will forever go with you. Let me know how you have been doing and what else I missed since we last spoke. I want to be sure that you get this asap, so this is all for now. Please write as soon as you find time, and if you have any, send some pictures (even if you do not like them).

Love Lance

    P.S. yes, I still have the painting LaLa.

2-21-2010 Sunday

Love Live Life

LaShanna,

Hey Ms. Lady, I got your letter today, these niggas came in with this brilliant idea to do mail on Sundays now. I ain't know that you moved until you wrote because when I called your number, your mom answered so I figured you were still on Storms. It is a relief to hear that you have not had children yet because everyone I know has children as well. Now let me catch you up on a few things. Remember the chick I was messing with when you hit me up on Myspace, and she responded to your message? Well she put me through so much shit, cheating on me and me being dumb, I kept giving her chance on top of chance to show her I really loved her, hoping things would change. I got her pregnant, she had an abortion. Then after I caught her cheating yet again, she left me. Can you believe that shit? Me and my mom's had a big fall out and she packed my shit and put me out her house. I ain't speak to her until a year and a half after that, but we are back on track now. Umm what else, oh yea! the last time we spoke, I weighed 379lbs. I lost a little over hundred pounds since then. I'm looking good than a motherfucker, and my dreads are down my back. I see you are involved, and by the way you speak of him, it sounds like you are in love. That's deep. What's up with your big sister, has she settled down and started a family yet, or is she still bugging. Not much else has change for me since I have been gone. Every day is basically the same routine. I hope you still write your poems when you find the time and haven't given up. I spoke to my mother and she said the two of you talked but she ain't get the chance to give you my address. So how you find me? I hope you ain't go on that website and see that busted ass mugshot I took because I look guilty as hell. It is good hearing from you. You have always found ways to help me through the misery that came to pass. I am going to check and see when we take pictures again, so I can send you one. Tell your mom's I said hello as well as your sister, I do not fuck with water boy like that and he will not remember me anyway. I will write again soon, take care for now friend.

Lance

3-5-2010
Love Live Life

LaShanna,

I got your letter the other day but I ain't respond due to lack of stamps, so sorry for the delay. You are crazy for what you said about ol'girl. I figured you ain't really like her from the gate. Anyway, I really don't know what made me stick around through all that bullshit, because you already know I ain't beat. Young love is so full of promises, yet ignorant of reality. My mom's said she remembered you though. She left Jersey City two years ago because they gave her an office in Union which is closer to the house. So damn your mom's about to give water boy the boot huh?! We'll let her know I am available and reviewing applications (let me stop before you curse me out). I cannot believe Meerah! What is up with her? Maybe it is because she is either too mean or she gay on the low (think about it). Well on another note, not much changes where I'm at, I'm just waiting for this shit to go by, so I can get my ass home and handle my business. My father be coming to see me here and there, but I still ain't fucking with him. He got married and had another baby, so there is seven of us now. I meant to ask if you are living by yourself and if you are driving yet? And how is your grandma down south doing. I have had a lot of time to self-evaluate and think on shit that I have been through. Which brings me to this, I have been there for others to depend on for most of my life which is why I am unable to understand why no one except for my mother is consistently here for me the way I have been for them. I have also noted you as my equal and no one else so in your opinion, answer this for me honestly. No disrespect to your current love interest but, we have known each other for damn near ten years and we practically grew up together. So why when we became of age, did not try to pursue a relationship with one another? Is there some flaw in my character or something that turned you away? (just curious). Oh, shit what happened to your cousin, I forgot her name, but you use to call her on three way sometime? It's mad niggas from J.C down here, but if they ain't M.O.B, I don't fuck with them. You know me? Well LaLa let me get this in the mailbox before shift change. I will write you again soon and I will stay out of trouble for now.

Take Care
Love Lance

4-9-2010

LaShanna,

Hey Ms. Lady, how are you? I just noticed how long it has been since I write you last. I just wanted to be sure that I ain't offend you with anything I may have said because it was not my intention. Anyway, not much has changed with me since we last spoke. My father has made his way back over to my bad side (long story). Well I am not going to make this long, so I will stop here for now. If nothing else, this letter should at least let you know that you were thought of.  Lance

4-22-2010

LaShanna,

Shanna What's up? I wanted to send you a response sooner, but we've been on lockdown. So they stopped the mail for a minute. Well, My Dear, it was good to hear from you after that hiatus you went on. I have a hearing scheduled for next month on the 12th for a sentence reduction, so hopefully things work out. Now back to the situation at hand, you are about to be a what, I know you ain't serious. When I read that I was shocked, I mean wow! I never expected you to have kids before I did. So, have you told your mom's yet? Are you going to keep it? And how are you feeling? damn that was mad shit! Anyways, yes, I'm hanging in there, no choice right? My mom is good I spoke to her the other day. Well Ms. Lady, I must get ready and leave for work, so I will end this here. I just wanted to get a response to you ASAP. I will write again soon, so take care.
Love Lance
P.S. Congratulations Mommy to Be

9-30-2011

Song: Goapele Closer to my Dreams

LaShanna,

It is always a very pleasant surprise to hear from you. The last letter I sent to your Jersey City address was on last Mother's Day and since I never got a response, I figured you wasn't beat. I want to congratulate you on a successful birth and let you know that I am happy for your situation. As you can see, I am not at the other address anymore, and Shanna I honestly don't think I'll be here for that long either. As a matter of fact, I was in lock up the day I got your letter which is why it has taken me so long to write back. I really don't want to project my negative feelings onto you, but it has really been tough on me lately. The more time that passes, the less of myself I recognize. This place is making me bitter and it scares me that I may be a worse person leaving than I was when I came in. My family is doing okay. Actually Shae (my sister) also gave birth to a baby boy in March, so I'm am an uncle now. As for my mom, she's okay, just dealing with some family drama; not to mention she fractured her wrist and foot (she fell off the ladder installing cameras at home). You know what I think that is what troubles me most, I mean

they come see me every now and then and they look older especially mom's, and subconsciously I feel like me being away is what is aging her. Well enough of my drama, what is going on with you and why did you end up moving? Oh, yea how is Mrs. Brown and that loser Marcus and is your sister still man-less? As soon as we take pictures, I will be sure to mail you one. I've lost so much weight, it's crazy! I went from 379 to 224. Damn! I almost forgot to tell you that I cut my dreads in February. Anyway, Love, it was good to hear from you and I hope you can find the time to write again. Until then, take care Sweetheart.
Your Friend Lance

12-7-2011

LaShanna,

This is just a short note to let you know that I did receive the letter you sent me in September and I also mailed you a response shortly thereafter. So, I figured it might be a good idea to send something else in case you never got my letter. I do hope everything is okay with your family and everyone is good. My mom's came to see me the other week and brought my nephew along, so it was good to meet him for the first time. Well anyways, Ms. Lady, be sure to write me, so I know things are okay on your end, and please send pictures if possible. Be safe and take care of yourself.
Lance

12-22-2011 Thursday

Song: Whitney Houston Step by Step

LaShanna,

I got your letter a few minutes ago and from the bottom
of my heart I am very sorry for your loss. I really am
Sweetheart. I won't sit here and say that I know how you
feel because it would be a lie, and I wish there is
something I could say to help lift your spirits. I do
remember your cousin, but I was unaware that she had a
sister. In any case, you and your family will remain in my
deepest thoughts and prayers. Damn La, it really messes
me up to know I'll always try to be around if you need to
vent or curse someone out (like the old days). Anyway,
though I see you mentioned moving again, where are you
trying to go and what brought about the decision? I have
also been meaning to ask is your family relocating, as well,
or just you, the little one and his dad (yea I'm nosy)? Well
this will be all for now and I hope everything begins to fall

in place, so you can have closure and heal in the ways you need to. In case it takes a while before you write again, have a Merry Christmas and a Happy New Year. So, until next time Shanna, please be careful out there and make some time for yourself. Keeping in mind that you are loved and wherever you may go, that love will forever follow.
Lance

2-1-2013

Happy New Year

LaShanna,

This is definitely a very pleasant surprise and when I realized it was you, I started bugging. What a coincidence I was just telling someone I wanted to write you but was skeptical because in your last letter you did say you intended to move. I must say I'm shocked that you moved all the way down there, but it sounds like you like it better. So that's all that matters. Damn, I wrote you like twice before and since I ain't hear anything, I figured you weren't beat, or something happened, but I'm glad you made some time. I'm a bit confused about your mom's and water boy's living arrangement, but I can put two and two together. Shit, I never really liked him anyway. On another note, my family is doing okay. Since I'm ten minutes away from home. I usually get a visit every weekend. My sister is working my mothers' nerves and she is about to give her ass the boot. Things are good though with them. I am trying to adjust because so many changes are taking place in my absence. As for your boyfriend, I really can't give an opinion and it would be biased anyway, but if he won't step up, let him step off. Now about this picture you saw of me I am curious. But since I am sure it did me no justice, I'm sending you one I took a few weeks ago. Wow I really ain't think I would hear from you again, but you always seem to remain in the back of my mind somewhere. It's so crazy how much time has passed; It doesn't seem that far from the days I use to sneak and call you. The good thing is I'll be in a halfway house in another twenty months if I stay out of trouble. As you can tell I am at this facility a second time. Anyway, Shanna I would like to see how you look these days and the little one, as well, so please send a picture or two. I still have one of you in your hallway on your birthday that you sent me back in 2000. So, My Queen, this is all for now. But it was good to hear from you finally and I'm glad you and my extended family are doing good. Please tell your mom I said "Hi" and I will tell mine the same. Hopefully,

I'll hear from you again soon but regardless, you are thought of and your absence does not go unnoticed. Take care love, I will speak with you another time.
Lance

2-21-2013

LaShanna,

I am finally getting this letter from you and I see you wrote it a few weeks ago, but for whatever reason I just got it. Umm for starters, I have this one picture of you from freshman year I think. No, it's not on the wall. It is in my photo album lol. You watch too many movies! Initially, I was bit offended by what you said in that regard, but I respect your situation and I would never do anything to make things difficult for you. Plus I'm not exactly the show and tell type. Here is what I'll do, I'll send you the one I have and hopefully when you are ready you will send it back, maybe with some company. There are a few things I wanted to discuss with you though. Although you moved and are making the necessary sacrifices to maintain your household, you seem so unhappy. I just want to know what are the missing pieces to see if I may be able to help in filling those spaces because I care. I never told you this, but I learned so much from you. You are from an era in my life when things were so simple, and I was happy. I just felt I should show how I appreciate your effort even after all these years (almost 15 years). Damn, we are getting old. As for my nephew he was just here earlier this morning. He will be turning two in another two weeks. I am glad though that this chapter is almost over. The only thing now is figuring out what I will do once this has passed. I'm not sure if you watch tv like that, but there was some show on MTV called "Catfish". Once I figured out exactly what it was about, I was like "damn! I wonder what Shanna would think of this?" There was another piece of your letter that stuck out. It was very sweet to know someone still cares about me genuinely. Yeah that's dope. I am curious though how you are adjusting down there? What do you do? And how do things look because I've never been there. About that Facebook thing, I still have no idea what my page looks like and it's crazy how you took a shot at my dreads lol. I'm having second thoughts about letting them grow out again. Other than that, I'm taking it day-by-day, so I don't hurt nobody. Seriously though, if you ever need some advice or you really need to talk, I'm here, even if I may not be comfortable with the topic. Well aright, Love, this will be all for now, but I will always respond whenever you write.

Oh yeah, mom's said to tell you "Hi" so "Hi". I will talk to you soon Shanna, thank you for the smile.
Lance

P.S.. Shout out to the box letters lol and to me not having electricity for three days. Shout out to that Digiorno pizza I know you burned lol.

3-6-2013

Song: Nas Cherry Wine

LaShanna,

Well I just got your letter today and it felt good to know that even though you have your hands full, you are still managing to make some time for me. I was also very surprised about the pictures but, I leave nothing to the imagination so let me say that I still think you are beautiful. Every time I see you, it's like the first time. Now about your accident, that shit is ridiculous and maybe you should go ahead and take her ass to court. Hopefully, you got a police report and took pictures of the damage. On another note I'm not really feeling the whole police thing because I don't want anything to happen to you. But it is a very good job, so I say go for it. It's a bit ironic how I was in the process of interviewing for the Sheriff's Department because I passed the exam, and only to get arrested in the middle of the process of everything. So, about the boyfriend situation. I know we are all not alike, but there is no way I would have my lady and son living as far from me for any lengths of time, especially when it appears as if she has made all preparations and all I must do is move. I don't want to get too deep because I don't want to make things awkward. But I am naturally protective of you and I don't think what you are asking for is too much. I will say this though; I want you to be happy with whomever you decide to share your life with. The crazy thing is I feel like if he got his act together, I may not even hear from you like that because it may cause a problem with, you. But it's a sacrifice I will unwillingly accept so you can have your happy ending. Now let's get to my drama (sorry I am cooking and writing lol, yeah, I cook). Okay now homegirl would drop in occasionally, selling me a dream about how she misses me and all this bullshit playing mind games, then fall off the map for a year. I guess those were the times her relationship was rocky. Anyway after doing all that, she sends me some random letter over the summer saying how she met some nigga and how amazing he is and how she doesn't want to keep leading me on lol. After all these years, then tried to make it seem like I was in the way of her and him moving on. Shanna I was so hurt. I mean that girl put me through so much foul shit when I was home. But my dumb ass kept holding onto the possibility that she would change. I must admit that shit made me a little bitter towards females because I'm a good man. I'm family-oriented and I'm loyal. But it seems like only the niggas that aren't shit, get the good ones. Whatever the case, I'm just so glad that this is almost over, and I'll be out in a few so I can get on with my life. You mentioned that God not being ready for you to have something, but giving you options. And I want to believe that so bad, this place has sucked so many emotions from me and I need to believe in something. Oh yeah, I'm not sure if your brother explained the phone situation to you, but we must add all numbers to our phone list every 90 days, so they can be approved, and they can't be cell phones, so let me know what's what, and I will get you on there asap. And what's up with you watching Lifetime? Every time I watch that channel either some chick is getting raped or its some other wild shit going on. I'll stick to "Bad Girls Club" and "Love and Hip Hop". You wouldn't believe I still watch "Baby Story" every now and again (OMG) that's crazy after all these years! Well, Shanna, this will be all for now and I don't want to keep you waiting. Check it though: when we are near the end of our journeys, hopefully our paths always cross. If you have nothing else, you have a friend in me. Sometimes in life, blood isn't thicker than water. Have a good night, I will speak to you soon, Love.

Lance

P.S. Check you out and your light skin friend. (Matching sneakers) yo her purse bag is hell.

3-19-2013

LaShanna,

What's up Shanna I got your letter today and I ain't want to delay in getting you a response. Please excuse my writing because I am very sick, and I am currently using the little bit of strength I have to write you. There are a few things I want to discuss with you, but there is something I need to ask you. We are both grown adults and I'm sure we have a very clear understanding of one another. Please keep in mind that I am in no way confusing you caring enough about me to correspond with me vs me having romantic intentions. This has always been in the back of my mind and I don't need to add anymore 'what ifs' to a list that is already too long. There are some things that you are looking for in a man, the qualities that I'm sure you know I possess. And I want to know if you ever even explored the possibility of something happening between us or if you are permanently content with the way things are? Whatever your answer is it won't change the way I think, feel, or act towards you. But at least I can close that door in my mind. Anyway, that whole argument shit is crazy and even though I would have handled the situation different in that aspect, I ain't gone kick his back in. How does your mother feel about him though? because I am sure she has questioned his presence in you and Taylen's life or at least his lack thereof (damn this shit is so sloppy). Whatever the case, there is something I really want you to do for me and although I am just grasping the concept myself, it is reliable advice. We sometimes allow our faith in people to block our common sense. We also allow ourselves to fall in love with our thoughts and ideas of what a person could be instead of being mindful of their actions. So, in any situation, please believe a person to be whatever their actions reflect. What the fuck! my throat hurts so bad! Anyway yeah, the only way I can call you is three way, so give me some time I will arrange that. I am sorry about this chicken scratch lol. Oh, I applied for college and did the whole orientation, so I should start in September for the fall semester. This is so random, but I've never been

to N.C. You should take some random ass pictures and send them. Listen Momma, I can't write too much more, them pills have me drunk lol. Seriously, though I look forward to your response in the meantime don't hurt nothing.
Lance

Undated

I hope your lack of response isn't because of the question I asked. If it is, all I can tell you is not to read too deep into it because it is only a question. I do have to be honest though. I do feel somewhat offended, but I'm going to leave everything where it is. Have a Happy Mother's Day in case you don't write.
Lance

5-5-2013

Song: Case Missing You

LaShanna,

I am so sorry, Sweetheart, and hopefully this letter reaches you before you tell me off regarding the one, I just sent you. See I've been waiting to hear from you since like almost a month now and because I never got a response, I began to feel like I may have made you uncomfortable by the question I asked. and you just ain't want to write back. I am just getting this letter from you today and I see you wrote it at the beginning of last week, and I feel so dumb. Now since I've explained myself, let me respond to a few things you wrote. First, I would never for any reason want to stop you from communicating with me ever. You are the only person who will ever have as much of my heart as you do, so nah it's not even like that. I really hope the job interview goes well for you, and see, as upset as you were, I told you the case would work out. Secondly, I probably should not admit this, but I am happy that you let that nigga go because he does not deserve you. I really did not like to say too much about that because I don't want to complicate things by getting my feelings involved. Anyway, though yes, I am feeling better and doing alright, things can always be better. Okay Love, look I don't want

to make this long because I want you to get it ASAP. I will be waiting to hear from you, and I'll be waiting on the pictures as well. Talk to you later, Shanna, please be safe down there… love you always.
Lance

P.S. Answer the question though, "have you ever seen those qualities in me (just curious)."


5-14-2013

Song: Babyface What if

LaShanna,

Damn Love, you know how to make me feel bad; I will take the blame for this one because I felt a little abandoned after not hearing from you. Oh, and the letter I wrote was so short and straight to the point because I wrote it like five minutes before the last mail run for the night. I am very upset though about not getting that letter because of the raw emotion you write with; I know you won't be able to recall every line word for word, so I would've appreciated having it. Since that is out of the way, I want to be able to open up a bit about something. I have always loved you, LaShanna, since we were children and if at any point in my life you would've came and said you wanted to give us a try, I would've immediately dropped whoever to be with you. As we got older though, it no longer seemed like you had interest in me like that, so I began to let go but never completely. You have a son now and I am in the situation I'm in, but such is life, and I believe the foundation we have, supersedes all of that. We have always been a team and that to me, outweighs a lot of things that would cause others to part. I don't want you to feel like you are just latching onto anyone because you are single, but if this is even something you want to be confident in knowing, you have a man that is willing to learn and love you in any capacity you need him to. Now let me address the updates…

1. Please don't feel too down about the job, I wish you would've mentioned this years ago because it is way easier in NJ. I took the law enforcement exam, passed and was being considered for two positions. However, during interviewing I caught this case. Be encouraged, Sweetheart, it's not over yet.

2. How much does she owe (the lady)? Either way, keep doing whatever you need until you are compensated for your damages and/ or court fees?

3. Put his ass on child support because at least it will be a court order that is set so he can't decide he's mad at you one day and not pay for the little one's childcare.

Trust me, it is only a measure of added security on your part, so I would consider making that happen.

4. How ironic! we got the phone update sheets today, so I will add the number so it can be approved. I will also set money aside, so I can pay for the calls myself, but keep in mind, I won't always be able to afford it. I will be calling as soon as the number is approved. Five Thirty and 6pm maybe an issue because we don't come out until after 6:15pm (we'll work it out).

5. Do take pictures and send me some. I know you probably have an iPhone, so find a mirror, throw on that cat suit I like, and strike a few poses lol. Nah I'm joking (unless you really have one). I brought a photo album just for your pictures a while ago and you have 93 spaces to fill.

Well LaLa, that is all for now, but I do look forward to hearing from you, I miss you sometimes, you know. Be safe though My Love, I will write again soon.

Lance

P.S. Damn you smell good, I am reminded that some parts of my body still work (wink). Seriously though you smell nice.

5-25-2013

Song: Usher Here I Stand

LaShanna,

I was just thinking about you, so it is a pleasant surprise.
Believe it or not, I do miss you every now and then. This
is going to sound so corny, but you really smell damn
good, I would advise you not to wear that when I am
physically able to be around you because it turns my light
on. It is very unfortunate that you had somebody like that
so close to you that never was really a friend from the
jump. Shit if we were in contact, I would've ruined that
friendship. I'm good at that lol (shout out to Cierra). I still
can't get over homeboy though, but you know they say
you never really know someone until after a few years
pass. It does upset me at times because I never picture us
going contrary to the plans we made as kids. But I am
grateful that we have remained in touch over the years.
Your presence in my life is a welcome one and you remind
me of a part of my life when I was happiest. I still

remember the first time I ever called your house, exactly what I was doing now, and your mom's asking me mad questions, then she getting on you for giving me the number (smh). I remember when you made me cry. I never told you why and probably won't, but you were my very first heartbreak. Nevertheless, I cherish all the long days and nights we spent together, on the cordless lol. Whether we end up together as we should have been or whether we stay close friends, I don't want to spend my life without you. You will always be my Sweetheart. Now getting to the red flags with Mr. Not Right, he was definitely bugging, but I guarantee it was because of whatever he might have been doing behind your back. All that calling your family checking for you (smh)! that shit is wack! One thing for sure, if he ever does put his hands on you, I am going to take him off this planet. It is a positive that you relocated because now you have a clean slate, and if I visit do not tell me where Zell or whatever his name is staying at (thought I forgot). I'm going to chip him like your mom's chipped Meerah that night. Things are going to work out, just keep doing what you are doing, Love. I have no idea where exactly to start when I get home because I missed so much. I never went through the party and clubbing stage, sleeping around was never my thing so I don't regret missing that. I know one thing, I hope your couches aren't leather and they are comfortable, so I can come through and kick my feet up

lol. By then you should know how to cook more than Digiorno. All jokes aside, Shanna, I appreciate you for being there for me even when I did not know it. In a perfect world, I hope you know how I would prefer things even with Taylen in the picture. So, I'll be waiting for that time to be right and I'll keep your voice in my mind always. Guess what? I'm listening to the radio and some of the songs we use to listen to when we were younger are playing (yeah that's dope) "♫ *Who make you rock your (body), start the party, It's got to be my man HiTek and Kweli*"♫ (remember that). Well alright, Love, I will end this here for now, with a smile on my face, love for you in my heart, and appreciation for having you in my corner.
Lance

P.S. I just realize I wrote this in print (smile) Where are the pictures, big head? And yeah, even though you be slacking in ya macking sometimes, I still love you and wouldn't trade you for the world.

6-4-2013

Song: Anthony Hamilton The Best of Me

LaShanna,

Good afternoon Love, I am just getting your letter today and since I have been looking forward to it, I am very happy to receive it. It also feels good to know your days are brightened a bit when you hear from me as well. And yes, I love the way you smell, it has been driving me crazy. Back to the topic of when we first met, yeah, your mom's liked me, but I had to grow on her first. But as far as your sister is concerned, we were always beefing. She used to be leaving me on hold mad long, then she would interrupt our conversations talking about she needs to use the phone. (lol) Truthfully, she ain't start being nice to me until your mom's put them paws on her. I must admit, it does feel good that we are rekindling that old thing. But if you ask me, the chemistry was always there, even in your absence. As far as a career path, I think you should consider applying for a position with an armored car service like Brinks. The job pays very well and it's kind of like you are a cop because you'll have a gun, and at least I won't have to worry so much about something happening to you. If not, then give me some ideas of what you would be open to doing and we will take it from there. So, let's talk about your paper issues (lol) I don't mind that you wrote on this and I am honestly impressed at how you wrote so neat like it was lines on it. Plus, it is better than that other stuff you use. That paper is so old the edges be brown like you got a stash of notebooks from when we were in middle school. Nah for real though I wouldn't care if you wrote on a brown bag, Sweetheart, that you make time to write, is all that matters to me. So, you think about me at work huh (licking lips). I must be moving up in your world! Let me stop because I can hear you now talking about some "Oh please boy", lol. To answer your question, "NO" there is no time off for good behavior because I have 85% sentence, especially not with the way I've been cutting up. Now I would've been on my way to the halfway house next year, but since I've been being me, I won't be eligible to go until 2015 summer sometimes. Which if you think about it, sounds like a waste because I max out exactly one year later. For the record though, are you saying you have or will be waiting for me? I'm just asking Boo, and I know you are smiling right now. What you mean nobody cooks on Fridays and Saturdays? (shitting me), we shall see about that unless you gone make one date night and the other family night, so we can eat out. I love the grandeur and bougie spin you tried to put on this garlic parmesan meal. Like you ain't just boil spaghetti and slap some garlic powder and parmesan cheese on it. I think it's dope that you have the food magazines because you have always been very creative, lol just make sure you do all your practicing now because you won't be experimenting on me. Also remember I do not eat vegetables and haven't over eight years. So I will teach Taylen some tricks, so he can hide his when you aren't looking. Also, who told you about the hook ups. Niggas only eat that in the county, but don't worry I'm gone make you something fly because even though you are talking trash, you know you want to try it. Yes, I can cook, should you be so lucky to have me make you breakfast, hamburger helper, or anything microwaveable. You will never doubt me again lol. As far as the books goes, you would have to buy the book and have the bookstore send it to me like Barnes and Noble. You would not be able to buy it, take it home, and mail it to me. From there, it can only be shipped from the source of sale or vendor. I am looking forward to the pictures as well, after all, I've only been waiting forever. Nah, I really want to gaze upon you and admiring your beauty. You want to hear some weird shit? I have never been to Walmart because I am loyal to Target. However, since I been away, I've been feening to shop there for some reason. On another note, homeboy is such a fucking idiot, but we won't dwell on how much of a deadbeat he is becoming. Shit you should put that ass on child support if he appears to be playing games like he is just trying to maintain some type of control over you. Look Shanna, I know you be working, and you hold your own but if worse comes to worst, tell me what everything cost, and I will make sure you get half. Never feel like you are pushing Taylen on me. How can I truly love you and not love him as well? Fortunately, or unfortunately depending on your feelings and point of view, I am not responsible for helping to create him, but you know what, LaLa, sometimes in life blood ain't thicker than water. My intentions with you have always been pure and I'm always open to building a life with you and we can build brick-by-brick as we go, because nothing is perfect. I only want to be sure that you want this life with me regardless of the bumps in the road for the rest of your life. Check you out with this talk of bubble baths and wine (smile). I remember we would be on the phone as you took your baths and read your magazines like some Hollywood superstar. You know I got you though. Before I forget the number was approved, but since you never said exactly when to call I haven't. Remember, we don't come out until after 6:15pm Monday-Sunday and I know you don't want to be at your mom's house waiting on me so let me know how we can arrange this. I also put a few dollars on my debit line so the cost of the first two calls will be on me. I have been okay though. I even started jogging for 35 minutes four days a week to occupy myself, so I have no energy to get in trouble. My mother will be down there this week in Gastonia. I asked if it was close to Raleigh, so she could drop in on you, but she's never been there. So she don't know. Anyway, Sweetheart, it was good hearing from you, and I look forward to getting another letter from you soon. Please be careful down there and when things get too quiet around the house, just know in all those moments I am thinking about you, LaShanna. (Sorry I wrote sloppy).

Lance

P.S. You always had a way to make my heart smile (thank you) I blow 3 kisses to the moon each night...one is yours.

6-12-2013
Song: Monica For You I Will


LaShanna,

I have been thinking about you so much since I wrote you last and even though much time had not passed, I started to miss you. I think a lot about your laugh, the sound of your smile (yes Sweetheart the sound), and the chattering sound that you make when you are starting to get bored or annoyed. I really wonder sometimes which of the two is more agonizing: knowing the feeling of having you in my arms, the soft caress of your lips and your touch, then having it all taking away from me? Or having to imagine all those things and not knowing how they feel as I do now?

Anyway, Love, I did get the book you sent me yesterday and I went through its page-by-page wondering if I was supposed to answer those questions or not. After really going through it all, it made me really appreciate you so much more and showed me that you do love me in some aspect. So, thank you for thinking of me enough to send that. I will wait on further instructions from you, so I know whether to write in it or not. And since it is so personal, I would honestly prefer us to do that together.

As soon as I got your letter today, do you know what I did first? (checked for your scent) lol. It wasn't there, but I was glad to hear from you anyway as always. Even though we lost touch throughout periods of each other's lives, I never forgot about you because you were always in my heart. I had to have my wake-up call too because briefly, I did think my ex was my soulmate. But she wasted no time in showing me otherwise. I am very glad you ain't get "that" tattoo and even though it wouldn't have been a deal breaker I would have been very jealous. I am kind of jealous now knowing someone who did not deserve you, could get so close. I am not going to ask how you burned yourself with you being the MasterChef and all, but I hope it is feeling better by the time this letter reaches you. And I'm glad Taylen isn't leaning on it like he usually does when you write lol. And you need to relax running around on the basketball court like some hooligan. I do feel bad though that you hurt your ankle (my poor LaLa). I owe you a foot massage and one kiss on that foot. You still never told me exactly what day or time to call. I would really hate to call and your mom answers. That will be so embarrassing, calling from a place like this. Other than that, things have been going okay, and I am grateful we continue to grow individually and collectively. Damn when we finally get where we want to be, this will make for one hell of a love story don't you think? I have two questions for you, have you given any thought to other career choices you may want to pursue? And even though this question is random, do you want any more children? Well Ms. Lady, I will end this here for now and I really appreciate you writing even though you have a few injuries. In case you were wondering, I always pay close attention to details when it comes to LaShanna, so I did not miss the message on the inside of the envelope. My life and what mean most would never be the same if I did not have you in it. Baby, I have always loved you and I won't even let you go, Sweetheart. I hope you aren't offended by me being so straight forward, but I can't wait to show you how special you are to me because your value is immeasurable, and I hope to have you eventually forever. Goodnight Shanna.

Lance

P.S. Nothing has ever felt as good as what I feel when I think about LaShanna…. Nothing

6-14-2013
Song: India Arie Nothing but Words

LaShanna,

I really am not sure on how to begin this letter because I am not sure today is real, the way you have me feeling now can't be expressed with words and this must be a dream. I got both letters today with the pictures of you and Taylen and it feels like Christmas, as silly as it sounds coming from me. Taylen looks so much like you. It is kind of bugging me out, but he is handsome like me (men don't say cute). As for you though, Sweetheart, you are so beautiful to me. You aren't my skinny Minnie no more, but trust I love the way you've blossomed (damn you look good). My favorite picture is the one with you sitting in the park with the little one on your lap. I know for certain that I want that package in my life, both of you. I see you still have your own style; you are all women. Hair done, nails done, everything done…

It's so crazy, after all these years I still never met anyone like you, Shanna. The complete package and regardless of what you say, some people are perfect. I am staring at two perfect examples as I write this letter. It took me all of 20 minutes to figure out you were in wax museum. I was really tripping for a minute. Anyway, though this week has been a little rough for me, but you have made my day for the third time this week. Whatever I did to deserve the thoughtful attention you give me, I hope I keep doing it. Damn I think I may be nervous to speak to you. Almost as I was the very first time, I heard you voice, I'll never forget that day. Since you said to answer the questions in the book, I will do so over the course of the next few days, then I guess I will ship it to your house unless you say otherwise. I am sure you know there are certain questions I won't be able to answer because we have not yet shared those experiences, so I will leave those blank. However, I do look forward to being able to fill in those blanks later down the line. But you can't lose the book, Big Head. On another note, how has work been going lately and how is your ankle and arm feeling from last week. This is so random, but you sent me two pictures of you up close, and LaShanna, I swear I could stare into your eyes forever. Just as I am doing now (flawless) I could eat you alive, I'm not being fresh. Okay, aside from that, I was happy to hear from you. I'm still trying to come up with something else you can do because you work some long ass hours. I still can't get over Taylen. I know he way bigger than this now. Check my boy out and he has good hair. While we are on the subject, you still ain't give me the status on his sneakers and summer clothes so make sure you let me know. Aright, Shanna, I'm about to go jump in the shower so I will end this here, so you can get it quicker. What's crazy, I was eating one of those oodles and noodles sandwiches yesterday and just bussed out laughing once I realized it because of your little joke the other day lol. Well I will be eating this once I get home too unless, of course, you are going to cook for me every now and again. So, Sweetheart, this is all for now. I will be thinking about you until I hear from you again. Thank you for sending the pictures (finally) and more importantly for you being special and making a difference in my life. Have a goodnight, talk to you later, loving you always, and never letting go.

Lance

P.S. I forgot you had pretty feet and I'm digging the yellow on your nails only you could've pulled that off.

6-21-2013
LaShanna,

I am just getting your letter today and I am somewhat relieved because I started to think maybe the ones I sent, never reached you I'm not sure how to feel about all this bullshit going on with you and Taylen's sperm donor. I don't want you to be concerned about anyone's opinion as far as him making himself to be a victim, especially when none of them are paying your bills or making sure the little one has everything he needs. If his sorry ass really wanted to be in his son's life, he would have brought his dumb ass down, there with you and handled his business as a man should. Honestly, this pisses me off especially because I've known you way longer and can only recall you crying maybe 2 or 3 times, yet this motherfucker causes you to hurt like this. This is the last I will say because from what I see happening in the long run, it is the soundest advice I can give. He is going to manipulate his dealings with Taylen and use the disagreements with you to do so. I suggest you put him on Child Support, LaShanna. So, when he decides you have pissed him off and he won't do for the baby, you will have already taken necessary precautions. Also, if you have not arranged a custody agreement, you should. Do not assume because you are his mom and full-time guardian, you are automatically in control. I would rather you have it written by a judge in case homeboy wants to play games. Now about the phone, I will not be able to or modify any numbers on my list until August 15, 2013. So don't worry about it for now. I did call your mom's number last week and it does not allow collect calls anyway, which means I would have to pay for the calls on my debit line or a prepaid account would have to be set up on your end. This will most likely be the same procedure if you get a house phone and for me to call all the way down there is going to cost at least eight dollars or more each call. Shit, it costs six dollars and change to call Brooklyn and I'm closer to New York. Like I said though, don't stress that for now because I don't want to be a financial burden or cause you any inconvenience. On another note, I filled the whole book out in one night, I stayed up until 3am last Sunday morning in the process, but I got it done. By the way, Love, yes the ink is blue, and no you aren't going crazy. Anyway, there are some very intimate questions in that thing. Only thing is after I send mine, how will I get yours? It's going to kill me if I must wait until I get home. So please feel free to divulge the juicy details and yes, I'm being fresh. I got the three wallet pictures of Taylen and I have no idea what happened over the past few years, but he no longer looks like you. I am looking at them as I write searching for any traces or resemblance of his beautiful mother, yet I see none. I do like the Jordan's though I always wanted them exact ones so snatch me a pair of 12 or 12 ½ when possible. Oh, yea stop talking about my sandwich. They were serving some straight bull, and I wasn't eating that. Wait, so are you going to make us breakfast, lunch, and dinner every day or only when you feel like it? I'm asking now so I can have my noodles on standby. I also got the thoughtful note and they made me feel good. Not many people have called me special and I know it's honest because you are the one saying it. I agree with you saying wait on God's time because I don't want to ruin what I have with you and it has taken so long for us to build what we have. I just want us to be on the same page and moving at the same pace and most of all, for us to be available when the time does come. I can't hide how angry I am at the way you are feeling, but always remember I am here for you even when you can't touch me or see me. Well Ms. Lady, I am stopping here for now, but my love for you will forever go with you. I love you, LaShanna…Unconditionally.

Lance

P.S. Smile for me Sweetheart, things will get better in time. I will add you to the list as soon as I can. Taylen called me that huh, he had the right idea, let him live (I don't mind unless you do).

6-27-2013

Song: Styles P feat Angie Stone Black Magic

LaShanna,

Good Evening, Shanna, I got your letter a short while ago,
so I am writing you back now. I know this sheet of paper
looks a little trifling, so you will have to excuse me on this
one. Well congratulations on the Cisco interview. Yes, I
know a little about the company because I peek at the
stock market channel every now and again. Also,
congratulations on the potential position with the
Sheriff's Department, I am glad that things are going well
for you in that aspect, but I am sure you will understand
that I am not exactly enthused. As you know, I am
supposed to have the badge and cuffs instead of State tans
and shackles so that news is bittersweet, kind of like a
reminder of how much my life sucks compared to what it
could have been. Anyway, I like the description of the

house because it suits my taste, but do you really need all that space? Lol There are only two of y'all for one thing. Or I should say there are two to consider. They have homes that you can rent to own, I'm not sure how the process works so you will have to consider it. But my aunt got this big ass five bedroom in Atlanta that she is renting to own. Secondly, Shanna buying a home is very serious commitment so be sure to consider whether you will want to live in the area or state for at least ten years. If you know for certain that North Carolina is where you want to spend the rest of your days, then okay. But if you have any doubts, weigh out your options. Damn LaShanna, I don't know what magic lamp and genie you found, but you need to let me borrow that shit for a while seriously. There was something I wanted to mention to you, but it has escaped me yet again, I must be getting old. I feel kind of guilty about you having the house phone because I don't want to add to any financial burdens. Anyway, I won't be able to call until the end of August because that is when we will be allowed to submit new numbers on our phone list. This isn't going to be a long letter. I am in a negative rut right now and this is mentally and emotionally draining. I try not to write you during these times, but I can't hide this side forever. Anyway, I am ending this now because I do not like the vibe or the directions this is going in. Take care though for now, Love, I will write again soon.

Lance

P.S. I ain't forget the book it will arrive shortly after this.

7-8-2013

Song: Musiq Soulchild Teach Me How to Love

LaShanna,

I am just getting this letter from you and before I get deep into what I want to say, there is something I need to make very clear to you and keep in mind since this is a very sensitive topic and it's you, I will explain instead of serving you like I would have done anyone else. For the record no I never lied to you. So whatever crap you read on Google or whatever, is inaccurate. And instead of providing all findings in my case, it has only provided the half ass police report. So, I will say this, yes there were two cars, the Dodge Intrepid is the one I was picked up from my house in, The BMW is the car these niggas carjacked and were going to take me to work in. Since my mother was home when I was picked up, she can explain to you that I am no liar. Secondly, I have all copies of any legal material you want to see so you know I have not lied to you. Think about who I am for a second and what I had going for myself at the time. I had my own car, a white Intrepid to be exact, I was attending college full time, I had a job at Lowes five days a week, and I had just taken the New Jersey Law Enforcement Exam and was awaiting my results. So, with all that, do you really believe I would have intentionally gotten myself involved in some dumb shit like that? So again, I implore you to further investigate before you openly assume, I lied to you. Now all this may come off like I have an attitude, but that ain't the case it just shocked me to hear that from you and you are one of very few that I will willingly explain myself to. Now onto other parts of your letter, I felt bad after I mailed it to you because I started to feel like I could've worded some things different. I was and still am glad that things are working out for you. It's just that one part touched a nerve and I was already stressed over the bullshit I deal with on a day-to-day as it is. So no your happy letters don't get to me Shanna and regardless of what I'm going through, I always look forward to hearing from you. It's not that I don't open up because I don't trust you. It's just that I am usually in a negative state of mind in here, so I don't want to be writing you and every letter be negative. So I leave those things out until they build up. However, I do have a trust issue with you. Since I been locked up, I would hear from you maybe once or twice, then you would just up and disappear for a year. So yes, I am apprehensive because I don't know when something will change, and you decide you don't have time for me. Most of my life, I have people who I love and thought loved me say they would be here for me and never hurt me and turn around and do the opposite. And to be completely honest, I felt like you were holding back from me. When you started writing again sometimes the tune of your letters made me feel like you were unsure of whether you wanted to invest time in me. Like you were straddling between keeping me in the friendzone or trying to build something meaningful. So, I am still getting use to be this way with you and it does make me nervous that you could change your mind on a whim. I would love to hear you say that you are in love with me and want to spend the rest of your life with me, and that you want to give me a family. Then for me to witness you taking the steps to make all of this happen, but that is in a perfect world. On another note this prison is not like the one your brother is in. There are no trade programs and things like that because he is in a youth facility. This is a known gang prison; they don't want niggas doing nothing but watching all this cable to keep us from killing each other. This process has made me kind of bitter, but it won't turn me into someone I'm not. It just makes me unconcerned with hiding the side of me that people don't know about. When I am angry, I turn into someone else, so I try to keep it all in check, but baby I need a break. I understand and truly appreciate your concern and I apologize for making you feel like I'm pushing you away. I just really don't know what it's like to have you so close (beyond the cordless) and I want to. So please have patience, dealing with me is not going to be easy. It has taken years to break me into these pieces, so it is going to take time to get me back together. One thing is certain, I don't know how to fix me, but we will see what happens, I guess. Seriously though, Sweetheart, do you really want to walk away from? Be honest. Could you be without me and be okay as if nothing ever happened? There is so much more I want to say, but I don't want this to be too long, you know. I am going to hang in there and I love you LaShanna. I want to know your answers to some of the questions I answered in the book. In the meantime, let me know If you started at Cisco and how things are going?

Lance

P.S.. Take pictures please, updated ones this time.

7-18-2013

Songs: Usher Help Me
        Joe Can I Be your Man

LaShanna,

I am finally getting your letter today and I have to say damn it's about time. Before I go further, let me get the drama out the way first, it is bad news. I got the decision from the courts last Friday and basically used a polite ten-page memorandum to tell me to kiss they ass and they aren't reversing my decision. On top of that, I was escorted from the unit I've been on for almost a year and put in lockup. These niggas going to tell me they not giving me a change, but they are putting me here for temporary housing until another bed is available. (You know I was pissed). Shit, I was fine where I was, but now I'm in the dungeon lol waiting for them to find or do whatever to get me the hell out of here. Now onto your letter, you may not have wanted to discuss what you were going through that upset you when you wrote me this letter. However, time has passed, and I want you to tell Sweet Daddy what's wrong. I know you're laughing. To clear up a few minor doubts, I need you to know that it is not possible for me to feel different about you. If we decide to be in a relationship, there would be no reason to cheat. Most men want every woman to satisfy their one need, I am a man that wants one woman to satisfy my every need and if whatever reason she can't or won't, I would just move on. I have known you for so long Sweetheart, too long for you to filter the ways you really want to express yourself to me, so I will tell you what I think…What you want is to tell me that when I get home you want us to start building our relationship. You are willing to work with me through the bullshit of starting from the bottom, but you want me to come down there, so we can be together. And that you really love me, and you are willing even now to commit to me for the rest of your life. Now, the reason you won't say this to me flat out is because you are unsure if I have those same feelings and goals in mind, and don't want it to seem like you are more eager to be with me than I am with you. You, My Love, are also a little bothered by the stigma about men coming home from jail, meaning I will be trying to make up for all the time I lost over the years by running the streets and sleeping around and this is not the case. I may be completely wrong about all or some of this, but we shall find out. As far as my plans when I come home, I owe Jersey five years of parole, but I want stability LaShanna and my stability includes a family and a decent job and a wife who will cater to me without question the way I would for her. For future reference don't say you want a man to come home to or to have quality family time, say who. On another note, I want to know how the job training with Cisco has been going? and how Taylen is doing? So, you know I think about you all the time and even though I haven't heard your voice in over 5 years, I still can pick you out of a crowd. Please continue to be patient, I am learning as I go along to be open with my feelings. Oh yea, I ain't tell her or ask her to tattoo my name. She did it after she cheated on me, basically manipulating my emotions to keep me around.

This may not be exactly the best time to mention it, but it would mean the world to me if you had my name. I would know that the gesture is sincere coming from you. I want you to seriously clear your head, think on it and honestly tell me, LaShanna, exactly what you want from me and worry about what I'll think my next statements may come across a little awkward since we never really discussed making love but listen…all you must do is tell me how you want it and I will give it to you just like that. I don't know how big you prefer your men, but you let me know and I'll tell you if it's in the cards for you or not. But the main thing for me is knowing you are enjoying it. It is hard for me to believe you never had an orgasm, but I owe you one (it's on the house). I have absolutely no problem at all with pulling your panties down, laying you on our bed and licking and sucking gently on your pussy until I feel your thighs tremble around my shoulders. I am going to take my time with you when I do that because I want it to be special for you and I never want you to forget that moment. Let me quickly change this subject because my body is starting to react, almost the same way I know my cookie in your underwear is tingling (yes, I said my cookie). If there is anything you want to discuss with me, please be open and ask. How about you? Let me know what your plans are when I come home. I also forget to mention a suggestion: just cut your son father completely off because you really do not need him. If I had my way, he would sign over his rights because I intend to make sure the little one is well kept. Well, this will be all for now. I know this letter was kind of long and you have better things to do, plus I want you to hurry up and respond. Two quick things before I go, make sure when you respond, you cover all the things throughout my letter, and you aren't distracting by our son leaning on your arm (he's mine also). Secondly, so you aren't in the dark about anything, there is a random lady who I hear from every now and again, professing all this love and grandeur ideas of what a relationship with us could be. I take none of it seriously and have been enjoying the entertainment and ego boosts, but that is where it stops. LaShanna, you have always been my greatest blessing. I really love you and at the end of the day there will remain no secrets or lies between us. Baby, I know you aren't going to like it, but if you are going to be my wife, I need to do everything to remove any doubts, insecurities, or hinderances that may get in the way. Have a good night. I will speak to you soon. Lance

P.S. Don't tease about how I address you. That is part of me expressing my feelings. Do get to Walmart so I can have more pictures of you.
Do kiss Taylen on his forehead for me. Don't forget I Love You


Undated

No Song

LaShanna,

Well first things first, thank you for thinking of me enough to write me on my birthday and wishing me well even though you are three days late. So, I am reading your letter and it has put a lot on my mind, so much that I'm not sure where to begin or even if I will discuss every thought I have, so let's begin with what is important (Taylen). It really blows my mind how you created a life with this nigga and he blatantly exhibits how he really couldn't care less. See now I wish you would've just let me send that money when I asked because now you need it. Unfortunately for me, not only am I flat broke, but I also currently have no job and it will take a while before I am able to get any. I will suggest, no scratch that, I am telling you one final time (put his ass on child support). I want to make it very clear that I do not want to hear any more complaints about him not doing financially for the little one as he should because it will be your fault. Whether he has a job or not doesn't matter, I'm telling you, Shanna, I see where that whole situation is headed, and I am trying to save you time and energy. What happened to the car? I thought everything was okay or at least you would've had the money from when the woman hit you to take care of small repairs. It also sucks to hear about this shift discrepancy with Cisco. Hopefully, you can hold out until you begin the preliminaries for the Sheriff's Office. Now I'm really am unsure of how to feel about that kiss. I want to be pissed, but then again, we aren't together. But still, I mean goddamn! Whatever though, I don't have much to say about that so moving on. How is it that you wouldn't tat my name, yet someone else doing it was almost a deal breaker? It's kind of confusing. Anyway, though I am going to be candid with you about this next one so takes deep breath and accept what I'm saying exactly and not what your mind says. I think it would be selfish of me to say for you to stop living your life for me, I never did anything like this either and I'm not saying for you to fall in love with one of them country-ass niggas, but I'm also not saying not to meet new people. I don't know if you could live up to the expectations that I would require of you if you "did this bid", and I wouldn't want to lose you over some bullshit. For example, regardless of your friendship with whoever this person is, since I don't know him. And you have never mentioned him to me there is no way I would have been comfortable with you being around him. Then hearing that he kissed you and you did not immediately smack the shit out of him would have caused a serious problem with us. So just knowing the kind of person I am, I don't think it would be fair to ask that of you so all I can say is do what you feel until you feel different. Lastly, I like how you completely avoided the sexual innuendo's in my last letter. You scared? Damn my birthday really sucked but hey it's over I'm 26 now (big whoop). Oh, I won't forget to call this month once they allow me to add your number and it is approved. You still have not mentioned if your number can receive collect calls or not. I am going to ignore that stripper comment.... I love you.

Okay this is all for now. Just in case you don't have time to immediately respond I want to tell you now to have a very Happy Birthday, Baby. I will be thinking about you heavy on that day. Lance

P.S. So much on my mind

Having mixed emotions
Missing you
Horny ain't the word
Wish I could have my cake and eat it
I want to eat your cake too
Very indecisive now
Smile
Would like it if you were more submissive
Love you so much
Do you really think I'm sexy?
When you play with the cat think about me.

8-10-2013
Song: Teddy Pendergrass Voodoo

LaShanna,

I swear sometimes I wish I could remain indifferent to some of the things you say at times. Your presence in my life helps me to maintain the balance I need, but also throws me off at the same time if that makes any sense. I got your letter today and of course I am happy to hear from you, but disappointed about your physical exam. That shit is crazy because the one up here does not require that, if possible, consider corrections since it is way easier and safer as well. Well, Sweetheart, at least you would've beat me in sit ups everything else you would've got spanked. Then I would have taken you home and spanked that ass some more (wink). It's good that you aren't discouraged because you shouldn't be, plus you only failed by very little. Now about you losing weight. I don't know if I like that. I would really prefer you to stay thick not, that I know how it looks since you ain't send a nigga no updated flick. Hell, no I never heard that having sex makes you gain weight. So yes, let's talk about me and you. I told you I ain't want you to wait for me because I honestly think that if we do make it happen and you find that maybe I'm not what you were really looking for, you will resent me because you waited on me. While I am being honest with you, let me also admit that I am not sold on the idea that you are physically attracted to me. I don't think it's a dead end as you said because it's not like we are in love. But I'm not doing life or some shit like that. So, it has nothing to do with me not wanting you to be alone (not entirely anyhow). Do you think I want some nigga spending time with you, being close to you or making love to that pussy that you are nervous to tell me is mines anyway? Like I said though, you must do what you think suits you best. I am not scared to love you. I'm scared to show you that I love you, to invest everything in you and things go awry. Now about the whole tattoo subject, we just gone move along from that because things are complicated, I do not want to talk about it so on the next one. I see you are still against playing with yourself (rolling eyes) but nah I brought sex up because I wanted to know how you like it so if chance arises, I can serve you cause I'm a savage lol I ain't really into the slow stroking. I drill. You also don't have to tell me to take no cues because I am always ready especially if you rock the mic how I like it. You are funny as hell too I had to look "arrogant" up in the dictionary and yes, the more things about me you think changed, the more remain the same. Your roar may be able to match mine, but it takes you longer to bite so you better watch out. I must smock about this next topic because somehow, I already knew you wasn't going to let it go. I did not mention the young lady again because my only objective at the time was to make you aware of her presence. The letters don't come frequently as they use to but yes Babe, I respond like I do to everyone, which isn't many because I don't get mail like that. She started writing me around the time you resurface, I don't know the shit is complicated, but nothing I cannot handle. For the record, I would never intentionally or careless put you in a situation like that if you came to see me. Goddamn hood books. It is a relief that your car was repaired, but I have no idea what the fuck a camshaft sensor or pigtail is. Shit, it sounds like pants to a high-tech barbecue grill. As far as you moving yes, it is okay with me if the rent is not higher, and the area is safe. Did you ask me that because you were being smart? or Do I really have a say so in what goes on? We should be submitting the phone list next week or so Sweetheart, yeah let's hope the phone isn't cut off. Scrooge huh I can live with that shit! Scrooge had money, his and everybody else's. I will tell mom's you send your love. Tell your mom the same. I am curious about her response. I will not send you any letters without a song again. I got you baby! Well let me go for now, but know I am always thinking about you, LaShanna, and I love you more than words can express. LaShanna, you could never really understand how much I care about you and Taylen. I love you.

Lance

P.S. So did my last name look good on you? And there better be some pictures next time. Put my favorite panties on and snap away. And I'm not using no condoms on you, plus it would rip anyway because if you let me do it my way. I am going to fuck you really hard until you cry, and I will not stop until I get the results I am looking for. So, think carefully on what position you tell me you like cause if it's doggy style, you're in trouble. Are you loud? (trust me I don't mind), it lets me know I'm doing my job. I love you Baby and my kiss means something.

8-23-2013

Song: Rick Ross Mind Games

LaShanna,

I have been waiting almost two weeks to hear from you because yes, I worry a little when you take longer than usual. So, I am very puzzled to finally hear from you today and it's not even a page. I have no idea how or why you are confused because I have been very open with you about everything in my life including my intentions with you. I can tell by your final thought that you are thinking way too deep regarding that girl or you are feeling threatened by her and just won't flat out say it. When I said, "It's complicated", I was referring to my acquaintance with her, I never said "Baby, she is complicating the way I feel about you or that because of her, I am second guessing being with you. However this is how it seems you are taking it. I really can't believe how you are acting right now, LaLa. But you say I don't express myself, if I am wrong then I have absolutely no idea why your letter was so vague. You of all people, know me so you should know to be straight forward about what you think and feel. Things may not be as obvious as you think they should be, so let me know what is wrong, Babe. Well since this letter kind of threw me off a bit I won't make this long, plus I want you to hurry up and write me back. By the way, I put the number on my list, so it should be approved soon. Hopefully, your line accepts collect calls because if not, I will have to send you the brochure, so we can set up the account. Oh, and I like how you tried to give me that line about the pictures, but okay since you want to be like that. Damn, you really acting stank. You ain't even mention what you did on your birthday or nothing. And I told my mother about marrying you, and

she was laughing. On a very serious note, let this letter be the last time you give me a half ass "I love you", stop being unsure of the outcome or reaction and put your cards on the table. Tell me what you want and how we can work towards that. I don't want to hear the "right time" and notions like that because if I feel something is mine, I tolerate no contrary opinions.
Love Lance


Undated

No Song

LaShanna,

Let me begin by saying I am very sorry for the losses in your family, to be honest when we spoke yesterday you sounded like you were holding up as best as you could. I ended up getting your letter later that night so I ain't want to delay in writing you back. It's crazy how country some of your words are beginning to sound and you've only been there a year or so. See, we haven't talked in years and I still know how you are supposed to sound lol. It wasn't worth mentioning yesterday but tell me why my ex sent me some random ass letter on Friday talking some straight bullshit, yes, the one with the tat. Anyway, she gone say nobody compares to me still and she want me and believe we meant to be, the bitch is clearly nuts. So yes, I wrote back and told her she had plenty chances but chose to keep shitting on me, I don't want her now and won't want her upon my return. It was more detailed than that cause I wanted to list all the fucked-up shit she did to me even over the years so hopefully she leaves me alone. Other than that, I said I wasn't going to find your brother because we are both the same thing and I don't want to end up smacking his ass because he wants to be fake protective, I'm a grown ass man. As far as Alvin goes, I know he stresses you, but I told you unless you took my advice, I did not want to hear your complaints. So let's act like you ain't mention it. You still never told me what you were going to do regarding your personal life or lack thereof since you never sent a detailed response to my last two letters (clearing throat). Oh, check you out, you ain't got no worries huh? You know where my heart is? Okay, then get on your job. It's a relief you have a spot at Time Warner, only for financial reasons because we are loyal to Comcast over here. Taylen was a bit shy talking to me but honestly the reality of his existence still hasn't set in yet. Other than that, I'm still dealing with the same bullshit, hopefully I make it past these last few years unscathed. So, you know, if I have not mentioned it previously, I will be almost 30 when I come home, and I do intend to start my family immediately thereafter, who want to be 35 having they first child? Ain't nobody got time for that. Anyway, I'm gone send you the phone thing with this letter I trust that we will have the account set up before the month is over. Since you were tired, you probably ain't get the pictures, but I want some specifically that you take for me and I'm not saying Baby get naked, but stop being too nervous to show me some skin. Well I must get ready to eat this big ass bowl of cereal before I jump in the shower and get dressed for my visit. So, I am leaving for now, Shanna. Please have a safe drive up here and be careful. I love you too.

Love Lance

10-9-2013
No Song

LaShanna,

Ms., I be home after 9am when I finish taking Taylen to school and I called the phone people to allow collect calls. I've been calling your ass since 9:00am. It is now 10:00am, not to mention when your machine answers, the goddamn phone says your number does not allow collect calls, contrary to what you are saying. Besides I sent that brochure for a reason. So unless your service provider is Verizon, which will allow me to call directly, you need to open the account like I said in the first place. Secondly, I been writing you back and I already know about homeboy and his new car. I will tell you one more time since asking you did not work, 'stop talking to me about that nigga'. I don't have to deal with him for any amount of time regardless of who he supposes to be to Taylen. Truthfully, I don't understand why you keep allowing him to play daddy at his own convenience, but whatever. Speaking of the sorry ass nigga, what happened when you came to Jersey that gave him the impression, he could invite himself into your life yet again at his convenience? You know what, I already don't like the nigga for reasons that should be clear, but you seem to not take it as seriously as you should, and I am starting to believe you may just like the idea of being with me instead of the reality that it comes with. Then you tell me in your last letter, you are going out and you let some nigga keep you occupied, and you are going to live your life. Now I have no idea if you meant it the way I took it but if you are going to do you, then say that and we can take everything else out of the equation, if not, then you should construct your sentences more carefully. There are questions I have that you never addressed (read the letters I wrote before I found out you lost your cousin and uncle). On another note I'm not feeling your living situation and you need to move because if something happens to you, I'm gonna get Alvin, it is his dumbass fault that you are down there anyway. What type of place you live where random niggas can loiter in front of the house? you should've called the police on they asses (you need to move). I expect you to be gone before the New Year comes. Don't give me a hard time! To answer your question no my mother did not get married, it was a joke, where are the pictures I asked for? You know what? Forget it because it does not feel right to have to ask you. About this comment you made, you need a man to protect "me and my son", plus you are horny (you trying to play me huh). Let me stop for now because this is upsetting me again. I love you and will talk to you when you write again, I guess.

Love Lance

P.S. Make sure you answer the questions because I need to know where we stand, I never been the whatever happens, happens type of person.

10-19-2013

No Song

LaShanna,

Before I begin let me say I saw what you write on the outside of your letter about your cousin and I am sorry for your loss. Let me now warn you that what is to come, you aren't going to like, so you can read it and be pissed off or throw this away. First and foremost, do not say or suggest to me that I need to step up and do anything. Me wanting to be part of your life is a choice, not a responsibility that is my obligation. Secondly, if you are too fucking proud to get the temporary assistance from this government, so you can keep your nose in the air and say you went through life without it, then that shit is on you. Thirdly, if you review a few of my letters from a couple of months ago, you will see that I told you not to worry about putting the phone on because you made it clear to me you weren't in a financial position to do so, and while I'm on the subject, let me inform you that GTL did not cheat you. It costs money when you first set up the account (how would they make a profit otherwise). Now let me make this clear yet again, stop talking to me about your sorry ass baby father because if you put his ass on child support like I and I'm sure others suggested, your ass wouldn't be living from paycheck to paycheck in regard to taking care of Taylen. I also told you before when you said or posed the idea of waiting 3 years for me, I gave you my opinion on how I believed it would turn out. So don't throw that shit in my face like I begged you to do me a service. Then you have the nerve to say to me not to speak on what goes on out there because I have no idea. You are right which is why I only spoke on what the fuck you said to me. You also said not to concern myself or better yet, I am too concerned with pictures. You know what? You can forget I mentioned it because it won't ever happen again. Regardless of that bullshit smiley face you drew after the sentence I know you, so the emphasis is clear. LaShanna, you really pissed me off with this bullshit. Remember it was me who had 200.00 dollars ready to

send to you for Tay not sorry ass, but you know what you had too much pride to accept it knowing the caliber of nigga you were dealing with. I see you mentioned nothing about more people loitering by your door or trying to move so that must not have been as important as you made it seem. Oh, yea let me mention how much easier it would be if you sought some of that assistance that is so beneath you (how dare you). So, I'm curious what is it that you are doing for me since you said that shit like you dropped everything in your life to accommodate me. I have nothing to say now. I have no idea if you will respond but if so, please try a different method because I have known you too long to treat you like a stranger but if it is needed to get my point across so be it.
L.

P.S. I am beginning to get the idea that maybe I can't handle this whole 3rd party situation with you and Alvin after all. This is the last I will mention him or his son since you went through great lengths making it clear that it isn't my business.

Undated
No Song

LaShanna,

I wrote you almost two weeks ago and still have not heard from you. I'm not trying to be arguing with you, but if you've decided that you no longer want to be involved with me on that level or any at all. I just would like the courtesy of knowing. I don't want to keep sending you letters if you don't wish to receive them, but if another week or so passes then I will have my answer either way...
Take Care

L.

11-13-2013

Song: Jagged Edge Walked Outta Heaven


LaShanna,

Truthfully, I am surprised to be getting this letter from you today, since I hadn't heard anything from you, I could only assume things were over between us and just yesterday began to mentally prepare myself to emotionally let you go. I am unsure of why the prison would've sent your letter back but if you still have it, I want you to mail it again. There are some issues that we need to discuss if we are to truly move forward and grow together. On another note, the decision to stay with your mother is a smart one, so don't let your pride convince you that you've failed and can't stand on your own two feet. You were very short in this letter, so I am unsure of what exactly to say to you now. Also, I have not put any songs or date because in your last letter as well as this one, you have listed none either. Just to give you something to think on since I did not clarify my meaning when I said it, I do not feel like we are intimately connected, and I want to. No, I don't want you to say what you think I want to hear or for you to stroke my ego. I want to feel like you belong to me and only me, baby I want to feel needed, not to fill an absence but because you cannot be without me. I want you to feel for me what I have felt for you all of these years. It was easy for me to accept Taylen, but I wasn't prepared to accept what he comes with. I have so much going on in my mind constantly being pulled in different directions, and I need my better half to help me trust her intentions and I need her to trust mine. No matter how the situation looks without questions. I hope we can get a better understanding of one another so we can be happy together. Because I do love you, LaShanna. Anyway, at least you are safe regardless of your living situation. I don't have to worry about niggas in front of the house. So, you know I got another letter from my ex, singing the same song after I made clear I did not want to be bothered, but she hasn't written since so I guess she got the point, for now at least. Well this is all for now, but I love you too…I love you with every fiber of my being, LaShanna.

Love Lance

P.S. I always asked for pictures because it is the only way I can see you constantly, sorry that you felt it was selfish to admire your beauty.

11-22-2013

Song: Ne-yo Ms. Right

LaShanna,

Baby, I have been losing my mind since I wrote you last because your response seemed to be taking longer than usual and I began to worry. I am unsure of what you mean when you say I don't open up to you. I am trying to express my feelings in the best way I know how. I just really want the security of knowing you are my lady and I always will be. I want to have confidence in knowing you will be here with me and for me through it all, and I'm not referring to this jail process. LaShanna, I love you so much beyond even my understanding. I also extend that love to "our" son Taylen. I need to feel like a priority in your life. I want you to defend me in public and private through the most adverse conditions. A lot of niggas would never admit this, but we want to feel protected by a woman as well. So, I need to know that you not gone allow me to be disrespected by another female and that you would beat her ass if it come to that. When we were younger, I was very self-conscious of my weight and in some ways, I still am, and as much as I would've liked to start life with you back then, I never felt like you thought I was your type. I know I can handle our situation right now because how will we make it otherwise, but I believe there is room for improvement. So, I want to hear from you what you feel are some things we need to work on. I may have come across a little insensitive before, but, Sweetheart, I really do care about the things you are going through, but when I can see a way to avoid something and my advice isn't heeded, it bothers me. Now as it pertains to homeboy, you should know whether he is there or not. I will always take care of Taylen. I just really don't like the way he wants to be his father when it is convenient. Especially knowing I would sacrifice anything to be Tay's dad. He is supposed to be mine, LaShanna, regardless of how things played out, and I am jealous because he isn't (wow I finally admitted it). Now let's be realistic if, I came into our house and he was there. I would've tried to kill him and I'm sure you know it. I want you to explain to me what is happening. The part you said was too much. Baby stop saying you must wait years. I only have 2 and like 10 months left. Oh, I had to take a new I.D photo so my online mugshot should be different. But you mentioned traveling to see me and what do you mean, once I'm home or in here? And when do you plan on doing that? I want you to be open and honest with me about your intentions with me, Baby. Do you think we can be in a relationship now? Or do you want to wait until I'm home? Because I'm going to be mad if I find that you have been sharing my cookie. My plan is to give Jersey the parole I owe them and try to relocate during or after it is served. As far as you go, I want to be with you, I want us to have a life together. Baby, I want to put that ring on your finger the way I use to imagine it when we were children. I want you to love me how I love you, and for us to be happy and have more babies (yes, I said babies with an S). So, let's figure this out together, Sweetheart, so we can strengthen our foundation and have an understanding for one another. A marriage is between two people who are devoted to the happiness and needs of one another and putting each other before themselves. I want that for us baby. When I heard your voice for the first time in years, I smiled in a way that I haven't since the first time you said you loved me. Your voice is so soothing and it's sexier with your new country accent. I really wish I left your mom's number on my list so I could call you. The new lists went in today and your current number isn't working so I'll have to wait another 90 days. I miss you a lot, Love, there isn't too many hours that pass each day where I am not thinking about you. I am upset that you are sick because I should be down there taking care of you. Making you tea and bringing you tissues to blow your nose. I know you grown, but you are still my Baby Girl, and it's my job to take care of you. We should be in our living room watching a movie with you wrapped in a blanket cradled in my lap with my arms around you (I love you so much). Please do not say for me not to forget about you because I would sooner forget how to breathe than forget you, Shanna (know that). In your next letter to me, please take your time and let me know everything you are feeling and don't hold back either. Tell me what I need to do to keep that beautiful smile on your face and how I can convince you to spend the rest of your life with me. On another note, your P.S. has me concerned because it is not the first time you said something like this, about something happening to you. If someone is threatening you or causing you harm, you need to let me know because I'm not having that shit, I'm telling you now. Always remember that my heart belongs to you and you will reign in my heart as I remain in yours. I will end this one here for now, but I will lose my mind if something happens to you. I love you with all my heart and that love will never fail. Goodnight Babe

Love Lance

P.S. When he asked who I was, you should've said your husband, because trust me you will be my wife.

-Give Taylen a kiss for me

-I am working on getting you another picture

-I would like more of you and Tay if it isn't asking too much

-And you said your feelings were stronger for me when we talked (please specify) I love you and miss you so much.

*Where is my song on your letter?

11-28-2013 10:12am
Missing you

Song: Tamar Braxton On My Way Home

LaShanna,

Today is Thanksgiving, but it doesn't feel as special as I believe it should. The memories I have about the holidays aren't worth remembering and I wish it was different, Babe. I should be grateful above all else that this year is ending, but instead my mood is bittersweet because it is also a reminder that another year has passed me by adding to the time that I have been dead to the world. I have held this pen in my hand and stared out the window for the past half hour, listening to some Adele album (yes Adele), and thinking about you. Every song I hear now nowadays always has you on my mind, I love you, Sweetheart, and I hope wherever you are today and whatever you are doing, you're safe and thinking about me as well. Throughout this process, I believe I lost some of myself along the way. I've been so busy existing and surviving the past few years that I forgot how to live, how to enjoy life. I think I've been kind of stressed out because there has been a drastic increase in my appetite and I know I put on some weight, so after Friday I'll cut back down and lose it again. I wish I knew what it was like to feel you in my arms. The smell of your natural scent, the taste of your moisture (I'm not being fresh). I'm serious though, LaShanna, my feelings grow deeper and stronger for you with each passing day. You are a very special young lady and I need you in my life. I wonder on days like this, how our time will be together. Whether you will let me enjoy the football game or harass me to help you in the kitchen. I can picture you coming to stand in front of the television to get your point. Or straddling me and shifting your body left and right and my attempt to look around you. I really am hopeful about a future with you. Taylen and myself which says a lot because you know optimism has never been one of my strengths. On a more serious note, LaShanna, I am and always have been in love with you and I want to be here in all the ways you need me. Just teach me how. I am deeply sorry for the loss you have had to endure over the past year, but I am here for you My Love. You will always have me. With us both being stubborn about having our way, there will be some rainy days but regardless I will never break my vows to you by walking away (I'm still here after 13 years). LaShanna, I just can't equate in words what you mean to me. Anyway, Shanna, if nothing else, I wanted to write you and let you know I was thinking about you. Please do not stress so much about things not being the way you planned them, something better is on the way and so am I. So keep that smile on your face, Baby, my sun would not continue to rise without it. Do not tease me for being mushy with you because I'm learning to express myself and it is a side effect of being drunken in love with the woman of your dreams... YOU. I love you, Baby, and I hope to hear from you soon Queen.

Love Lance

11-29-2013

LaShanna,

See now things like this are what cause me to doubt the possibility of us being together and confuse me even more about the ways you say you feel towards me. Throughout this recent letter from you, you mention things and then contradict yourself in 2 or 3 sentences later. On one hand, you say if we get together now, you won't be happy. But then you go on to ask whether I want to wait to be with you when I'm home or be with you now? But it doesn't matter to you. Then you say if you do so, you will feel like your life is on hold and you don't want to waste more time if shit goes bad like in your previous relationship. Now put the shoe on the other foot, what if I waited for you until I come home, and then shit goes bad. Where does that leave me having been the one to put my life on hold for you? Now about you "fighting" you obviously misunderstood what I said which I don't understand because I broke it down for you, LaShanna. So how am I supposed to feel about your reluctance to defend me as I would you. How would you feel if some random niggas called you out your name in my presence or vicinity and the reason I give you for not defending your honor is because I'm not going to fight in the streets like we are in high school. But it's good to know the truth. Also LaShanna, I have absolutely no kids and have not been in a relationship for almost seven years, so what is this female problem you accuse me of having? Do not take this any other way than how I am saying it, but I think you have a somewhat unrealistic idea of what a relationship is supposed to be. But by the sounds of things, you seem to be treating me a bit like someone you just met and haven't known all these years. It's kind of like you separate me or are protective of things regarding my interaction with your son. Yet you require things of me that you feel are necessary to have a life with ya'll, so I don't know anymore. Now it probably wasn't your intention, but you hurt my feelings in how you constructed your letter. How I see it honestly, what I feel for you is more intense than what you feel for me as is constantly indicated by your caution with me among other things. You really don't seem to be considering my point or the sacrifices I am or would have to have made to be with you. Relocating is one of them. Also consider that I got locked up at 19 and to be with you, I would be immediately taking on a responsibility because you have a son, which I wouldn't have minded. But as I said, I have noticed how you separate the two of us. It's like there is you, Taylen, and his father. Then it's me and you, and I'm no longer sure about functioning as third place. More importantly, LaShanna I want my own children, meaning babies. You've known this as long as you have known me. Which means, if you do not want more children, which is basically what you said. That isn't an ideal relationship for me because I intend to begin my family at least in the first 2 years that I am home. You want to be married and I respect that, but how are we to immediately marry without even knowing if a relationship can work?

Mind you, I'll be 29 when I leave, and I'm not trying to be 34 and up having no babies and that subject is something I will not compromise on. The way you put things just has it looking one-sided and beyond your just trying out a new relationship unbeknownst of the outcome. I do not see where you are sacrificing much of anything. LaShanna, the way you have me feeling right now? maybe it would be best if we stopped all of this and just remain friends, because I played everything out for you. But you are too cautious and doubtful and keep finding ways to counter what I say. I am upset, but in a disappointed kind of way. But I guess I'll get over it. So, live your life and do what you feel you need to do in order to be content. But you don't have too much faith and there are too many contradictions, so I would rather just stay cool with you.

I Love You, Goodnight L.

12-8-2013

Song: Beyoncé 1+1

LaShanna,

Good Evening sweetheart, I have been thinking about you all day, almost every second of it, and wanted to write you another letter. It really makes me feel like shit knowing you are down there dealing with everything on your own. Even though you may have mom down there, it doesn't equate the difference I know my presence would make. With me being locked up and so far from you, it can add a strain on our relationship. So Baby, I know at times it may be a little tougher to deal with and So, I want to thank you for all the effort you have put into us building a life together. I appreciate the letters that you send me, as well as the time you set aside in writing them. Baby, you are truly an amazing young woman and I am proud that you are mine. I focus so much on the day-to-day nonsense and stresses in preparation for my return, that I have lately been allowing it to overshadow the two most important people in my life, you and my little one. Because of these sobering moments, I realize how ungrateful I can be sometimes, and I apologize Sweetheart. You deserve so much more than I can provide now, but when I am able, you know I will make everything right. Just please do not give up on us and even through you are being overwhelmed as of lately, keep that beautiful smile on your face. It will get better. I told you a very long time ago that you have a man who loves and cherishes you, and that will continue to love you in any capacity you need him to. And I meant those words. Nobody knows me in the ways that you do, Babe. You are an invaluable friend and you are going to be an amazing wife. I would marry you now if circumstances allowed it. Anyway, My Love, I hope things have become a little easier since your last letter to me, but if there is ever anything I can do, Baby Girl, please say it and it will be solid. I would like to know how things are going at your job and how Taylen is coming along in school? Did his school pictures come back yet? Oh, yea I remember you mentioning a few niggas at your job trying to get at you so you need to let them niggas know that your husband is on his way. And if they not trying to die or go to jail over you, keep it moving in that order. Damn it just dawned on me how quickly Christmas is approaching. See, I'm supposed to be at home with you decorating our tree and fussing with you about whether to put a star or an angel on the top. Well LaLa, this year is ending, and I am so happy to have been able to have you in my life another year. I look back over my life and I am humbled by the fact that you have always been here when I needed you the most. LaShanna, I can't live without you so no more threatening to cut me off, okay? Okay My Love, I did not intend to write as much as I have, but I wanted to share some of what I was feeling with you. I love you with all my heart and I am in love with you the same as I have been since we met all those years ago. Keep your head up, Baby Girl, I will be missing you and thinking of you until we speak again. Have a goodnight My Love.

Love Lance, your husband

P.S. Hug Taylen for me.

12-6-2013
Song: Toni Braxton feat. Babyface Hurt You

Baby Girl,

It was never, nor has it even been my intentions to add any stress you are dealing with, LaShanna. I'm not going to debate with you back and forth over this, but in your last letter, you said that you would not be happy if we started our relationship now and was persistent in inquiring whether I would prefer to wait until I was home or not. Under those circumstances, Sweetheart, how could I not feel the way I felt, because in my mind, I love you so much, LaShanna. And since I know I want you, I do not see the point in waiting until I am home. Whether you will admit it or not, you are a bit insecure because you can't fathom that I am in love with you enough to remain faithful to you once I am home and until I can relocate to where you are, especially being my age and in the place I have been in for years. From the time we were kids I always was faithful to you in your absence LaShanna (how could I change). I think it messed up that you would suggest I go back to an ex that's dying to be with me. I wouldn't expect such a low blow from you. You need to calm yourself down through. I keep telling you better days are near. It may bother you not to have been able to spoil our son like he deserves, but he is still young enough not to understand. Young enough to be satisfied with having cake with people that love him. I wouldn't be me if I sugar coated shit, but it's coming down to one of two options. Either put your pride aside and get temporary assistance or put that niggas on Child Support because if he won't do for Taylen, you need to keep him the fuck away from him, because what purpose is he is serving. Also, I never said you treated me like a third wheel. I said I feel like it because you keep this bum around and seem not to allow me the responsibility because you want to keep giving him a chance he clearly don't deserve. If Alvin wanted to take care of his child, he would be and he isn't. If it were me, I would've sold that fucking car and handled my responsibility for mines. So, we don't have to keep always discussing this topic. You should just let me know the stipulations you want regarding my dealings with Taylen because it isn't as obvious as it should be that I love him and would do whatever to ensure he is good. So, if you are unwilling to allow me to be his father in all aspects, let me know and I will stop bugging you. Now see how simple it was for you to say you would stand up for me. So why we had to go through the whole fighting like I'm in high school business, LaShanna? The only way I feel we won't work is if you do not allow me to be the man you know I am. If you stand by my side and stop popping shit and trust me, we will be fine. You need to make up your mind like I have. That I am yours and there will be no other alternatives. I want to be your priority, Baby, not a possibility or choice. Baby, stop fussing with me and tell me what I can do so you don't feel as alone as you do because it really hurts to hear you say that. How could you even contemplate not writing me if you assume, I am stressed which isn't the case! what does that say for our future? If shit gets rough Babe, it supposed to be until death do us part (so act like it). It's so boring to hear that it sounds so easy to walk away from me when I can't live without you. Sweetheart, I am sorry your toe is hurting and if you weren't acting so stank, I would've kissed it for you. LaShanna Robin Herring, I love you and I have always been in love with you which will never change. Baby, you need to trust my counsel and take my advice. I only want the best for you and my son. Yes, mine. I don't give a fuck what the birth records says. When it counts the most, I am still going to be here like I always was. I want you to be with me, LaShanna, now Baby, not 3 years from it. But part of your compromise is to let me be the man, allow me to be who I am. I know you don't want to feel like you kept Alvin away, but at this point, it is becoming essential (trust my intention). I want you to write me, My Love, so we can find a balance, I love you so much, LaShanna, and cannot live without you. So, take a minute to think about all I am saying and write me immediately don't keep me waiting. I be missing you so much as it is, and I do not like that you feel the way you do. Tell me what it is you guys need, and I will see what can be done. He is mine, LaShanna. I don't want to hear that shit about you feeling like you are pushing him on me. That little boy dwells in the recesses of my heart, the same as his mom. I love the both of you (you better tell him). Now let us put aside the nonsense so we can continue to grow together. I love you, please forgive my being insensitive. I never meant to hurt you baby.

Love Lance

P.S. You do not understand how devoted I am to you. Write back baby and do not worry, things will change but you have to stop focusing so much on what isn't going right. I promise you things will get better.

12-14-2013
Song: Adele One and Only

LaShanna,

Baby, I got your letter a few minutes ago and was very happy to hear from you. I swear that three days I usually must wait be taking long as hell. I'm glad Tay got the card and as promised it will never be late again because him and your mother-in-law have the same birth date. Don't be making fun of Pluto if our son recognized it. It is all I care about. It feels good that you and I are back on the same page and our balance has been restored. I have faith, as well, that we are going to make this work as well, Babe. I did not come this far to be without you, so I will never give up our relationship, nor walk away from our family. I am unsure of exactly what you meant in saying you hope I'll be ready to be really grown, but trust that I know what my son needs from me. And I know the man my wife needs me to be, so Baby, don't worry. I am grateful that at least Taylen will still be young when I leave this place because it bothers me when I think about missing out on important things in his life. Let me tell you a few things I have planned as soon as I come home. First, I need to go through the written and driving exams so I can get my license straight because its expired years ago. During those first couple of weeks, I must get the conditions of my parole established so I can map my wiggle room around that because I am coming to see you as soon as possible. Sweetheart, all I do is think about your sexy ass all day and being able to kiss those sweet lips and holding you tight for the first time. When we make love together, I will experience it as my first-time period because nothing before you matters, Baby and I am backed up. I imagine looking in your eyes when my dick is finally inside of you, where it belongs and where I have been aching to be all these years. I am going to kiss your body all over from your neck, past your collarbone, licking my way across your nipples and down to your toes. You are my queen and I hope I will be able to take my time because I want to bite softly and suck the inside of your thighs right before I lick your pussy. I like the way you strategically avoided the details of rocking my mic. And yes, I do like it doggy style, but I will do it in a way that you can still look at me. Damn LaShanna, I really want to have one hand on your waist and one on your ass pulling you slowly into my dick, while watching your sexy faces, hearing you, out of breath. I need to look into your eyes, Baby. I know you and I will have that connection (I think you are going to cry). I am open though to the changes you want to make. All you got to do is tell Daddy how you want it and that's how I'm going to give it to you. Don't forget I been gone away for a minute so that first round might be on the house, or it may not, but if you are on top, I know I will cum fast as hell. You know what, Love, the chemistry we share is amazing and has always been (even without sex) so I know when I make love to you everything will come full circle. What you mean you gone only marry me if I make you tap out, you gone marry me regardless. If you think about it, you've been my wife for 13 years. Starting way back when we use to talk about you having my twins. LaShanna, it is amazing how long I have loved you. No one ever compared to you or even took your place in my heart not, even if you were absent for a period. I always knew the day would come when you would be mine forever. Oh yes since you brought it up, please Babe, send pictures when you write again. I don't want to be greedy, but I want a lot and make sure you take some updated ones of you just for me. Shit I wouldn't be upset if you modeled a pair of your panties for me. I refuse to replay memories of my sexual past on or to look at strangers in some magazine when I need to ummm relieve some tension. I would rather look at pictures of my wife and think about me fucking her. I know you are usually busy, Sweetheart, so I'm not going to press you. But when you are able to make time, I do want more pictures of you and the little one. You have 87 empty spaces in your photo album. As far as Christmas goes, I honestly believe I have what I want already you and our son. But if you want to, just let it be something that will put a smile on my face. I just got a new job so soon as the money start flowing, I am going to send you some. Now that I know Tay likes cars, it makes it a little easier to shop for him. By the way, did you hug him and tell him I loved him like I asked cause if not, we going to box. How is work going, Shanna? And how are you doing emotionally? From day-to-day. I just want to make sure you are okay, Baby Girl, that's all. I know you get sexually frustrated these days, but I promise I am going to make it up to you. Trust, I will never get tired. I am going to make sweet love to you each hour, minute, and second as often as you let me. As for my cookie between your legs, she will be my breakfast, lunch, and dinner (I bet I'll make you cum). You have given me the motivation to get back on my shit, working out. So after New Year's I'm all in. Now about these mugshot comments, I let the one in your other letter slide, but don't get it twisted. These niggas in here know my history. Ain't nobody whooping my ass or taking my cornbread. I was sick as hell when I took that picture and early as hell in the morning on a rainy ass day. Your husband ain't no punk, or did you think I kept switching facilities by request? You funny as hell!. Anyway, I gained at least 17 pounds since I took that, I took a picture a couple weeks ago for you, but I know it look stupid since the nigga made me laugh and my collar was flipped up. Anyway, Baby Girl, it was good to hear from you, Sweetheart. You have been helping me make it through this shit. I love you more than you will ever know, LaShanna. You are the woman I want to be with and spend my life with. I do not want to go to sleep and wake up with anyone that is not you. You are all I think about day and night and I refuse to ever live without you again. This year is almost over, and I will be home before you know it and I will do whatever you say to that pussy. I'll do anything you want me to. I love you with all my heart, LaShanna. Please be careful down there, Sweetheart. I will call you as soon as I can arrange it My Love. Have a goodnight, Babe. I love you Mrs. Herring.

Love your, Future, Present, and Past Husband, Lance

P.S. What are some of your plans for when I get home? I want us to plan our future together. I Love You and miss you. Did you tell your mom we getting married?

12-27-2013
Song: Trey Songz Forever Yours

LaShanna,

How are you doing, Baby Girl? I just got a letter from you and the card you sent me with the pictures. Before I get any further, Sweetheart, let me tell you that you are so beautiful. I swear, every time I see you, it's like looking at you for the very first time. I also have no complaints about the paper you used. Shit, you need to steal some of that and take it home as crisp as that shit is. I'm not at all happy about Taylen not feeling well. And I'll bet it's all because that day he had on no jacket during the fire drill. Now about your preparation for my arrival, you tryna move a nigga down south huh? I would be able to relocate my parole, but you would have to be my spouse or immediate relative, Babe. Check you out, I'm glad about the child support situation because I was so upset with you about that. But it is another step in the right direction, Babe. To answer your question, there are plenty of things you can send besides books. Let me know what you have in mind. If worse came to worse, they would send it back. I wouldn't get into trouble. Just so we are clear on this in case I never flat out said it before I like my women thick, usually between sizes 10 and 12, and at least 180 pounds, all fineness. I was never into the skinny, petite, kind of chicks. So that flat stomach and all that, does not impress me. I need a woman not no little girl, Babe, so don't worry about any stretch marks. So, if that was the only reason you are hesitant, Babe, send my pictures and stop playing, Girl!. Wait I had to stop and look at your pictures again you are so sexy, LaShanna. I mean damn, Baby!. You will always have a sexy body to me, and I will absolutely love you in any condition, Sweetheart. All I can say about that whole ring situation is that son is a clown. Why is he even talking to your mother about things like that, anyway? Anyway, Babe I hope you were able to successfully get your Christmas shopping done and can relax because you sound so exhausted. You know what, you are truly an amazing young lady and I really admire the person you are. I appreciate everything that you do for me even in thought, I love you so much. I am always thinking about you: how you may be feeling or what you might be doing. I miss you just as much if not more and at this point, I have no idea how my life would be without you. Can't wait to hold you while you fall asleep at night. Now when you say you think we should get married, do you mean while I am here or what? Also, I don't want to hear 3-step programs unless you gone be taking birth control because I can promise you, I'm not going to pull out. Oh, yea Babe, there are no trade programs at this prison because it is a gang jail, I had a better chance taking a trade in

Yardville when I was there. About my mom, I say little things like here and there when we are squabbling like "Ma, LaLa acting crazy", but we never get in deep discussions. She knows I love you though. I don't know, my mom's different, Babe. Her whole philosophy is she doesn't have to deal with woman in the ways I will, so if I like it, she loves it. She's not meddlesome in my relationships. I will discuss a few things with her this weekend, but she has always remained indifferent except for this one time. If you show interest in having that mother and daughter-in-law type of relationship, she will reciprocate. Anyway, Sweetheart, I hope this letter reaches you with a smile, and you know I am missing you, like always. Oh wait, I got another random ass letter from my ex, talking a bunch of bullshit, asking if she can visit (yea ok). I just wanted to mention it because it almost slipped my mind. Why when I am finally happy and have the woman of my dreams, bitches want to fall out the sky suddenly. Oh, yea one more thing, Shanna, nobody says 'BJ' anymore. We can call it 'rocking the mic' plus if I'm going to be spending my food stamps, I want my change lol. Nah, on a serious note, Babe, I need it and it is more to it for me than just the sexual gratification. Damn, I'm starting to write sloppy, let me go. Baby, I love you so much and I thank you for the nice card you sent because it really made me feel special. Thank you also for the pictures. Do not forget to send more when you send my son's school pictures. I love you, LaShanna, you mean so much to me.


1-1-2014

Avant My First Love

Baby Girl,

Today is New Year's Day, my Love and as usual, I cannot get you off my mind. I spent the last few hours of last year looking at my pictures of you and my little one. You probably going to think I'm crazy, but every now and then, I look at Taylen hoping to see any physical traits of mine. If you decided to go out and celebrate last night, I just hope you were somewhere safe and made it home okay. Because I would lose my mind, LaShanna, if anything ever happened to you, Babe. Anyhow, I decided to start the year off with getting back on my workout shit, so I just went out and jogged for 25 minutes and took a long hot shower. My legs are sore as hell along with my shoulders and lower back, but after finding out yesterday that I gained 28 pounds, I had to do something. See I am in a tough spot because if I go back down to 220 you gone say I look like I'm getting punched on. But I don't want to get bigger because I worry that you won't find me as attractive so I don't know. I mean I know you say my weight isn't an issue for you but certain things you say convince me otherwise. Ultimately, I just want to look good for you, Baby, and only you, so I would like to know what you prefer. I really could use a massage from you right now though, and no, I'm not being fresh, unless you want me to. I have been writing you more often because when I say that I am always thinking about you. I really am. I don't want to overwhelm you so if it becomes too much, let me know. Anyway, Sexy, I really did not make any resolution. All I want to accomplish this year is for you and me to continue to grow together in love. You know I really did not have much of a fair hand in my life, but you have made this past year so different. All the years I have had you actively in my life because you're different. So, when everything is all said and done, if I can spend the rest of my life with the woman of my dreams, it will have made everything in between worth going through. I'm still thinking about you saying we should get married and have a wedding later. I would like that. You know what, Babe, you always have had a way of making my heart smile and I appreciate those moments. We have so much history, Baby, but the crazy thing is that I am still surprised at times when I think about how in love with you I am. I never know I had the ability to love anyone this much and I am glad that it is you. It has always been you Sweetheart. Just so you know, I am going to have that talk with your mother-in-law this weekend so don't worry, but even if she wasn't as supportive as I know she will be, it would never change the fact that you are mine and I am yours. Well, Shanna, let me end or better yet pause this moment in love with you for now because I want you to get this at least by Saturday. LaShanna, I love you with every fiber of my being and will always be at your side until my last breath. Be careful down there, Babe, kiss my Taylen for me and know that I am missing you and thinking about you constantly, My Love. I hope to hear from you soon, Baby Girl, I love you always.

Love your Husband Lance

1-13-2014

LaShanna,

Please forgive my delay in writing you back, there has just been so much nonsense going on that I have been unable to quiet my mind long enough to do it. On top of all of this, I have been as sick as a dog for almost two weeks. I can't even talk since my voice is gone. Okay, let me get this out of the way first. Baby I know you won't like it, but I am going to tell you anyway, so you know I'm not keeping anything away from you. So, tell me why last weekend my ex pops up down here? I go in the visit hall expecting my uncle and it's her. The exchange was very awkward, but I'm like I don't like you, so why you come? for closure or something? Then she goes on to explain about maturing from how she was when we were younger and all this other stuff. I know you don't want to hear it, so I'll spare you the rest. But I'm like you suddenly want to come see me now and all of this like what do you think is going to come from this? So, she says, "I know you been gone a while, so when you get home, I want you to live your life and do you but, when you done running around, let me know because I'll be waiting, but in the meantime, I'm going to be here for you as much as I can". Yes, Babe, I did tell her about you, hoping that would deter her efforts, but she seemed very unphased. Now getting to your letter, you have me very worried. Please calm down and separate the stressful things that are important from the bullshit. I want to know what you are thinking in those moments that caused you to cry. I was a bit confused since in your last letter you said you got someone to take your lease and you had a new management. So how does moving in with your mom fit into the equation? Even if you are staying with her, it is beneficial because you won't have many bills to pay which will allow you to save more. Okay now you also asked me about my parole situation, as well as, moving down there. As far as parole, I can only be paroled out of state with a spouse or immediate family member that has been in that state for at least 2 years. Now about moving, relocating is not my issue. I am just unsure about N.C and other redneck states, in general. Babe, things are going to be very rough for me since I have a felony and even a job at McDonald's is unlikely especially since I'll be almost 30. I am unsure if you can deal with me once I get in my "fuck everything" mood because you haven't yet experienced it. And with me having to struggle to reestablish myself, they may be frequent. Sometimes when you express your feelings for me, it still bugs me out because I never thought you would feel these things for me. But I love it and l love you too. Oh, yea this is the second time you've spoken about a male best friend. But why have I never heard of him if you know him so long? And I hope this ain't the one that kissed you. Also, I never got the chance to speak to my mom because we had a serious ass snowstorm and she was unable to visit, but like I said, my mom supports whoever I choose. It's not going to matter to her about you leaving and coming back, her whole point is going to be "so if shit worked with your boyfriend, you wouldn't be trying to deal with me in this way". And we would only be friends. So see what I mean? Oh yes, I can't receive paintings or nothing else like that! Hello I'm in jail!. I do miss you though, and I'm not liking having to wait all these days in between talking to you. I know you say you want the old LaLa body, but please don't lose the little bit of ass you have left. You are going to need some cushion to bounce your way from the front of my thigh as I pound you the way you need it. Well Sweetheart, I know this letter was all over the place, but I'm still woozy from…Sorry Love, they called me to another part of the prison to see if I wanted to register for this college semester since I dropped out this past October. I was having issues with the professor teaching style and quite frankly, I couldn't see how writing thesis papers was going to put money in my pocket. Even to think of you or Meerah finishing school and still having issues, bothers me cause it's like what's the point? This is my fifth time trying to do this college thing and even though the education is free, that doesn't seem like much motivation. Okay, Sweetheart, I cannot do this anymore because I can barely hold this pen and my head is spinning from that long cold ass walk, I just took. Listen LaShanna, please be careful baby and don't scare me like that. I worry enough as it is. I will be waiting on your next letter and thinking about you until it gets here. I love you so much, and you need to stop starving me, I am not explaining what that means because it should be obvious, so don't ask. And tell whoever took them pictures to get better light next time because you are blurry. I love you, Sexy.

Love Lance

1-25-2014
Song: Avant 4 Minutes
    Tyrese How You Gonna Act Like That

LaShanna,

You are really pissing me off and since you saw fit to
address me so formally and keep it short and to the point,
I will extend the same courtesy. For one, this is my second
time at this prison because they shipped me out back in
2010 when your ass wasn't writing. So, the visit list I had
then, was the same upon my return. So for your fucking
info, I did not know she was still on my list since I made
sure to remove her when I was in Bordertown. Secondly,
it is very childish of you to throw this bullshit tantrum
when I could've done like most niggas and lied to your ass
or just not mentioned it at all. Not to mention your ass
has been back to Jersey at least twice since I been back
here. Even after you told me to put you on my list and
how many visits have you made? Exactly! WHAT THE
FUCK I THOUGHT. Now about my mother, how many
ways can I spell it out to you that she doesn't give a fuck
who I am with so long as I am happy, bottom line. I do
what the fuck I want to do so I don't know why you
making it seem like me being with you is contingent upon
my mother's approval. I'm a grown ass man. Thirdly, stop
giving me the whole being a mom talk because even after

you had Taylen, you were still trying to work shit out with Alvin and I don't blame you. But don't say it like the only reason you ain't write because you were raising Tay, unless you lied in them letters you sent me back then. I'm not even tripping off that shit, so no, you won't have to bring it up again. But if you want to get technical about shit, you wasn't checking for me when I was home. You were living your life and again I'm not tripping, but don't say it like I been the focus of your attention all these years because I wasn't. And when I tried to get serious with you, you always seem to find some polite way to ward off my advances. Also, don't say I ain't look for you because I sent mad letters to that Storms Ave address, only to hear from you after being locked up for 2 years from a different address, after you just so happened to call and get the news from my mom's. None of this shit even matters because look at where I'm still at 14 years later, still chasing you. So think about that before you say this indirect bullshit you are saying in this letter. Let me make it clear, jail has not made me desperate and if I wanted that bitch or any other, I would have them and would not be pursuing anything with you. You are the one living in a whole new state with a family I did not help create. And although my number one rule is to not fuck with anyone with kids, my Love for you supersedes that, so you better choose your words carefully before you ever hit me with this jealous passive-aggressive bullshit, LaShanna. I'm not none of these soft ass niggas pretending to be something I'm not so don't insult me like this. If you want to keep on this path and ruin what I thought we had, then fine it's on you. I saw your little smart-ass comment, but I bet you can't tell me one promise I ever fucking made to you and did not keep. I been waiting long ass hell to hear from you sitting here daydreaming about your ass and finding out shit about NC so I can be with you, and this is what the fuck you have to say to me. I don't care how mad you are, you owe me an apology and I hope the tone of your next letter is drastically different from this one. You have a man dedicated to you, hopelessly stupid in love with your ass. We never even spent time together and I feel crazy about you and this is the fucking attitude you take? Don't you ever again as long as you choose to know me, compare me to anyone of them niggas you been with. Some niggas like stupid shit like that, I thought you knew me, yet it's apparent you really don't. You have no idea how it feels for me to realize you think I'm that naïve and stupid to ruin what we have after wanting you for so long, because some bitch decides to shoot me some random bullshit.

I ain't act like this when you had Alvin all in your fucking house taking showers and shit. I ain't push the envelope because I trust you regardless if you were telling the truth or not. I never questioned you. But you can act like this with me over a supervised visit with that bitch who couldn't touch me if she wanted to.

I keep telling you my plans so if they not suitable enough for you, then let me know. But let's keep in mind who is really making all the sacrifices here. All you are doing is writing. You aren't planning to move and take on a new responsibility, regardless of you never having time to live your own life. I'm saying this so you know I deserve more respect than you are showing me and all the more priority, as well, because I am always willing to prove that. But it seems you are always so willing to let me go, and I'm not feeling that I believe out of anyone I have ever been with it, it should be you who fights the most to keep me because of our history, especially when I make it easy by showing you, you are the ONE FOR ME.

L.

2-15-2014
Song: Usher Here I Stand

LaShanna,

This recent letter from you threw me off a little, for one, because I don't see how you could find anything about what I said funny, but I understand why you said you laughed. The whole shit made me mad because it is easy for me to question things you say and to believe you out there doing you, despite what you tell me. The hard part is to trust you 100% and have faith in the woman I believe you to be. But still and all this, is the option I choose. I hear what you saying about Alvin, but Baby, you know me, and you should also know the length of my sympathy. As far as that nigga is concerned, he should've slept in his fucking car since he would prefer to have it over Taylen. He could be one of them weirdo niggas, smelling your panties while you weren't home or rummaging through your shit. I just never want you to forget that I would put a bullet in anybody to protect your honor or guard your safety. Even when you feel it's not worth it, you are always worth it. You do not need to concern yourself with me changing the way I love you. As long as you trust me regardless of how crazy shit gets and never walk away or threaten to. I also need you to continue doing what you are supposed to do to hold me down and help maintain my peace of mind. I'm not being a smart ass, but I've never really been much into the talk. I like action and I want to see some more action from you. When it's all said and done, yes Sweetheart, I forgive you. But give me my due respect as your man and never again insinuate disloyalty on my part in regard to our relationship, Fuck That! Our Marriage!. LaShanna, emotionally all I want is you. I want your love unconditional, your deepest desire and every idle thought. This makes things difficult because of where I am since this is the part where I would carry you into our bedroom, lay you down, pull your clothes off and fuck you until you cry or at least until I am satisfied with your apology. On another note, I have been missing you and was worried since ya'll had a snowstorm recently. All I could think about was my baby in her car getting stuck in the snow with my son and me not being one call away as I should be. I also did not forget about the pictures I asked you for. I told you about your stomach not being a problem for me. How you think shit is going to be when you in your forties after you've pushed out 2 more of my babies? Yes, I'll still think you are sexy. Baby, do not make excuses. It's not like I'm asking you to get naked, so please do as I asked. I do nothing but obsessively lust over you constantly, so send pictures, more than four. How has Taylen been doing in school? and How is his behavior in the house? Also, be sure to include everything that is going on at your job. Oh yeah, we will be submitting a revised phone list for this quarter, so send me a number that isn't a cell phone, Babe. You can send your mom house number. I will put the first 40 dollars on to speak to you. This letter writing is nice, but it takes too long sometimes, and I want to hear your sexy ass voice, so figure it out. I expect a number with your next letter and my pictures. By the way, Christmas been past, so where is my gift, plus Valentine's Day is next Friday, aww man, you slacking. I'm going to let you go for now, Princess, but know I will be looking to hear from you real soon. I miss you so much, Baby. Keep in mind, I will not ever take you for granted, and will never play any games to get between your legs, that do not include my tongue. LaShanna, I love you Baby. Have a goodnight Sweetheart and make sure you blow a kiss to the sky for me every night before you go to sleep.

Love Lance

P.S. You never told me your plans with me, and make sure you overview this when you write so you touch on all bases.

2-18-2014

LaShanna,

Well now I hear from you, thank you for at least thinking enough of me to send a card. But receiving it, does not change how upset with you I am about the way shit is going with us, or should I say, not going. I sent you a letter two weeks ago and two weeks later, you send me a card. I know about the snowstorms that have been going on down there, but I guess it did not click in your mind that I may have been concerned huh? So being that you indicated you did not lose your job until Valentine's Day, what the hell was going on all that time prior to that? This does not feel like a relationship, LaShanna. I do not feel the affection or nurturing attentiveness I need from my woman that I know you possess. So, at this point, I don't know what else to say or do as far as "US" is concerned. This should come as no surprise because I remember raising these same problems a short while back. About your job, I really don't know what to tell you about that because we discussed the possibility of you losing it which should have provided you with ample time to prepare and make the necessary changes. I have no clue about the child support issue, but if you are getting it, hopefully it is enough to do what you need to do for your son. I told you about the phone shit in my last letter, but you never responded for whatever reason. When you get around to sending a number, it will be too late so forget it. I really don't know what else to say to you because the whole situation is beginning to piss me off. I made it clear to you what I expected if we got serious and how I would react if you began to falter, so I am only being true to what I said. I feel like I am by myself and not with a person in a relationship and I shouldn't feel that way. I spelled it out for you what I need and how to love me and I'm not seeing that you understand. Whatever be safe and I guess we will speak when we speak.

Love You Lance

P.S. A day away from someone I love, can never be special.

Undated
Song: Lisa Stansfield Been Around the World

LaShanna,

I got your letter the other day and had no intentions on writing you back, period. There was just a strong tone of finality in your words especially when you ended what you had to say with good-bye. This is aggravating, LaShanna. I thought you would be the one to remove the stress from my life and instead as of late, you have been adding to it. You say I sound like I did not want to be in a relationship. So if that was the case, why the fuck would I keep telling you that you aren't making me feel like we are together. Then you said I'm not there for you either, well if you felt that way, why you just now saying it? I try all I can to be part of your life. In my letters I always express concern for you and what you are dealing with. As I said before because I definitely ain't overlook anything. I wrote you and expected a timely response and I made it clear why. But since you dragged your ass, it was too late to add the number by that time. I got it like I told you it would be, your fault, not mine. I also don't like how you always make it seem like you are so stressed and so busy and never have time for yourself. Yet you find time to go out with your friends and make appearance in videos. I believe you are down there doing you, LaShanna, because the way you have been acting towards me is different. This does not, as a rule, mean you are fucking or in another relationship, but I do believe you are entertaining the company of other niggas. As you so vividly pointed out, "I'm not there for you", so if I'm only not there for you in the physical aspect that you imply, then someone else must be. I made it clear to you in the start what I expected from you if we walked this path, and I also made you aware how my reaction would be if you became inconsistent. So how you can feel any way for me doing what I said I would do, sounds crazy. I think it is very selfish for you to always act like I must adapt to your changes all the time. Am I not sacrificing enough? I just don't know what else to say so if you write and can fix this, then fine. If not, then that's also fine. I'm just tired of giving my love and getting nowhere. I want to feel like you love me the way you say, and I don't. We are supposed to be getting married and even with the strain on our relationship. I have to beg you for pictures and shit. I got to wait to get two maybe three letters a month from you. I deserve more than that, especially from you. But if you are incapable of stepping up, let me know and we don't have to play no games. But the way, shit has been going bad since the New Year came in, I don't like it.

L.

Undated

No Song

LaShanna,

I really am unsure of where to begin to be honest. I am trying to figure out exactly where I am or better yet where we went wrong? When and why did it start to feel like we were strangers to one another instead of two lifelong friends trying to build and maintain a relationship. The complaints I have been making to you about not feeling the affection between us have not been me just being dramatic with me on our relationship. Our only means of communication are through the phone, visits, and mail. Unfortunately, we can only use one of those options and that is also stressful because of how long it takes. You have to see that my hands are somewhat tied, Baby, so it is on you to step up and make more of an effort. I don't know what you are dealing with down there, but I have an idea. Still and all I made you aware of what I expect from you and I do not think I am asking too much. I never see you and knowing this and it seems you still have a problem with sending me pictures. We never speak. We could have but somewhere along the line, there was a miscommunication. So that is not an option and won't be for the next 90 days. Sweetheart, what I am about to say next is going to sound messed up, but I do not mean it in a bad way. So just let me make my point. There are women who I would have no problem getting mail, pictures, phone calls, and visits from on the regular if I so chose those paths. Women who I can guarantee have a lot more on their plate than you, but I want you LaShanna and I need you to make way more of an initiative then it seems you have been. Just the same, as I know you can easily be with a man where you are who can physically be around and provide for you in ways that aren't possible for me at the moment. So being that we both knew this coming in, I think there needs to be improvements made on both ends because if we cannot add to each other's lives, what is the purpose in us being here in any capacity? I believe a relationship is between two people who are willing to put each other's needs first, each compromising to keep one another happy and since I have not been feeling like this is what is taking place, I keep bringing it to your attention. But Babe, how long am I suppose to complain about the same issue, both directly and indirectly before I decide to walk away. On another note, I don't know what to tell you about Alvin because you should not be allowing him to visit at all. Also, I don't know what the hell makes you think I would be a good candidate for this "man to man" talk. I'm the nigga they call when they are tired of talking, so I don't know about that. Let me be a bit more candid

with you. I don't want to speak or even look at the nigga, so unless you want him in the ground, you need to find another way to not deal with him. I told you from the start, I'm not with the 'baby daddy' bullshit. Taking you as a package deal was for you and Tay, and not you, Tay, and his father. Well my hand hurts so I'll stop for now, but next time give me a bit more detail about the shit that is going on. Also, please consider what I said about our slow declining relationship because I want us to work, Baby, but I cannot force you or argue back and forth when you aren't handling me the way I should be. I love you and will hopefully hear from you soon.
Lance

P.S. let me know if I sent you a recent picture of me or not because I have one for you. I've been asking you for 3 months. If it's not gonna happen, just tell me. Imma be mad, but at least I won't feel like a dumb ass for continuing to ask you, LaShanna. Love you anyway.

4-16-2014

No Song

LaShanna,

This whole situation has been weighing heavy on my mind since my letter to you. The fact that it is a little past the middle of April and I wrote you last at the end of February, but have yet to get a return response, just further proves my point. The bottom line is that this is not working out between us, LaShanna and I am tired of feeling like I am putting in more of an effort then I am getting. Maybe this whole long-distance aspect on top of me being in prison isn't helping I would rather end this now then to eventually ruin a friendship due to failed relationship. I have complained time and time again about things that have not changed. So rather than resent you, I would prefer we be friends. Maybe our time has passed or maybe we can work when the circumstances are different, but whatever the case, it isn't working now. And I'm exhausted from feeling like I am forcing it to. I'm unsure how you may take this, but I doubt you'll be upset. There is no way you can convince me that this has felt anything close to an intimate relationship. Since I had trouble hearing from you thus far, I am unsure if you'll be writing now. So, if you decide you want nothing to do with me, I will leave you alone. If you would like to maintain our friendship, I'm cool with that too. I tried, Shanna, but between Alvin and the drama he brings because of the bond, I can never share with you, on top of me having to be the one to relocate and deal with all of that. I'm not sure I want to. All I see is where I'll be the one compromising and having to sacrifice. I do not see equal effort or sacrifice on your end. I do hope to hear from you but if not then, take care and I hope all works out well in the end for you....

4-25-2014

Song: Boys II Men On Bended Knee

LaShanna,

I got your letter a little earlier and there is one thing that caught my attention that I felt I need to clarify. Your exact words are "if you feel I'm not doing my part, then be happy with someone else", because since there is no "Someone else," I'm unsure why you emphasized that? Let me also let you know that I made my ex understand that I was married, and not only did I have no interest in her, but also made sure she was removed from my visit list. I'm just telling you this just in case you feel like my last letter had anything to do with her, because it is hard to understand why the love of my life would encourage me to be with someone else. Baby, it is clear that you aren't doing your part. I feel like I am constantly complaining about the same stuff and you aren't fixing them and making things improve. For instance, you just said you down there taking care of business and getting your shit together. The whole problem is that I do not feel included in any of that. And I have told you flat out so many times and it's like I'm speaking another language, you don't understand. I really can't agree with the notion of things between us not feeling right due to the distance because our whole experience together is bonded through long distance communication. You are right. I don't know what can happen 2 years from now, and one of those unknown possibilities could mean you ending up with another man. Is that how you would prefer things? Baby, look I have suffered in silence throughout our years while you have been in relationships with others, and I will never do that again. On the same hand though, if we are in a relationship and I feel like you are indifferent to me being here-- because of your lack of attentiveness and affection, where does that leave me, Hun? About the letters you mention, LaShanna, you ain't start being intimately open toward me until last year around this time. Before that, you were being strictly platonic, so what is it that I am supposed to discover through re-reading old mail. I hate that we are even having this conversation because you know I do not want to be without you, Baby. I just do not feel relevant or like I am needed and fuck the macho shit. I'm gonna tell you straight up, men need to feel needed by our women. So hypothetically, if we separated, would you really be able to live without me? Baby, would you really want to be happy with someone else? So, you know, since you think I be tripping over Alvin, remember when you told me you hated the fact that my ex came to see me, using the time that was ours to share. Well Sweetheart, this is how I feel about him, but I can cut and did cut my ex off. You have to be involved with him forever because of Taylen. I would love to be his father and nip homeboy completely out the picture, but you want them to have a relationship. But it pisses me off that he can just come down there and be around whenever he wants, even if he has to do it under the guise of spending time with Taylen. Yes, I am jealous since it isn't obvious to you and regardless of my aggressive personality, I do have feelings too. I'm not sure what else to say for now except that I love you, Baby. What now? Love me

5-5-2014

No Song

Baby,

I got your letter a few minutes ago and will submit the visit for tomorrow. It should be processed before you make it up here. You did not say whether you would come on Saturday or Sunday. I would prefer Sunday because my mom's usually come Saturdays, but if Saturday is the only day you can make it, please call my mother, and let her know to tell me so I can tell her not to come. Babe do not wear bra with any metal underwire, wear sweatpants so these hating ass females that work here have no reason to give you a hard time. Hopefully, you will get this before Friday, so have a safe drive if you are driving. Another thing, Sweetheart, I know you are not my biggest fan right now, but I want you to know I love you. I know I've been working your nerves because you don't say it to me like you used to. Hopefully we can establish some understanding this weekend, but seriously LaShanna, I love you, Baby, nothing can change that.

Love Lance

Undated
No Song

LaShanna,

Sweetheart, I am just getting your letter and honestly all of this stuff has me angry and worried. You never quite specified what exactly happened to Taylen. I really am not even feeling the fact that he was spending time with that sorry ass nigga, but I guess not much can be done about that so. I was really looking forward to seeing you and cancelled the visit with my mother to do so. And not seeing you was a disappointment. I gained like 30 pounds due to all this extra stress so maybe not having you see me like this is a good thing. You mention that there are some things that you wanted to say to me face-to-face, but since we have no clue when that chance will arise, you might as well tell me now. I expect it to be bad news since you worded it in that tone. Let me just say that if it has anything to do with us not being together, please say it now and don't wait. I have this number you sent, but of course, you did not say if it's a cell phone or house phone. Also, we only have 2 days to change our phone list and by time you get this and respond, it will once again be too late. I do not even know where I put your mom's number, but it really doesn't matter at this point because I do not have any money anyway. LaShanna, I do not know if or when I'll be able to get someone to call you on three-way, Babe. Remember, it costs $10 and no one is ever home at my house. Other than that, you have been on my mind and I do miss you, Babe. This whole process is just frustrating, and I am feeling like I do not have any options. Even you and I are in a weird and uncomfortable space and I don't know how to get us back to where we were. Are we even still together? Well I hope Taylen is doing ok and these words find you the same. Why aren't you sending pictures to me, LaShanna? I have been asking you since January and it's now 5 months later. Please don't write me without including an answer to that question because I'm feeling some type of way. Come to think of it, you sent me a book last year and I answered every single question and mailed it back. So I have to ask you, "Have you forgotten how to love me"? Well, I really don't know what else to say so I guess I'll speak to you later.

Love Lance

6-6-2014

Song: Sade By Your Side

Sweetheart,

I want to begin this letter by first telling you that you are so beautiful in these pictures you sent me. I want you to also know that I love you, Babe, and cannot wait to kiss your sweet lips for the first time. I really ain't digging that whole skydiving shit you were on, especially because you seemed to have made such a dangerous decision without asking me how I feel about it. I am, however, grateful that you made it home safety, Baby, because those was some slow ass days that I waited to hear that my Baby Girl was okay. You really be having me worrying about you, LaShanna. Now getting to your letter, you saying that you want me to be in good spirits does not alter the conditions that I live with every day, Babe, it isn't easy. As far as this praying stuff, I can't pray to an idea that I do not believe exists. I did all of the praying I'm going to do when I caught this case and it got me nowhere. If he, she, or whatever wasn't there when I needed it the most, now that it's almost over, wtf I need 'em now for? I don't know what you mean by saying "I want you to be in good spirits or we can't go on with a relationship"? But if you are supposed to be my woman and we are working on a life together, I'm not sure you should say something like that to me. Also Sweetheart, I need you to accept responsibility for your role in my life, because you failed to see that you are the only woman who I love, who I can depend on, and who can get me back in focus when I need it. If we are working towards marriage, LaShanna, it is your duty to be by my side through whatever I go through, regardless of my mind state. Baby, that starts now not once we have said our "I do's". Honestly, My Love, you confuse me when you elude to us not being together, especially after we both agreed we were going to make us work and never give up no matter what. Baby, what is it that you expect from me? I mean, you have known me almost my whole life and you are also aware that I haven't been dealt too many good hands. What I'm asking is if you know that all I have lived through is negativity, why do you expect me to act like shit is sweet and life is good. You play a huge role in my happiness babe and I need you. You are my only escape from this, and I need your support. I would like to hear from you more often than I have since mail is our dominant source of communicating, at least for right now. I also would like to get more pictures of you and Taylen since visits aren't convenient option for us all the time. I'm begging you which has been the case. I mean seriously, Love, I brought this 99-picture photo album last year and I only have 21 pictures. Come on, Babe seriously, I mean I know you are busy but am I really asking for too much? Anyway, it is good to hear you enjoyed your holiday in S.C and most of all, you are okay. You tell your uncle if something happens to my wife, I'm going to deal with him. About you applying for the Fire Department, I hope something works out, but I know you were more motivated by the salary than the position. On another note, I can't believe you cut your hair that short. What I'm gone pull now? I also see Taylen is getting bigger. He'll be five before we know it. Unfortunately, we did not get to finish our conversation, but I really would like to know where we are headed so it doesn't feel like we are just going with the flow. Baby, are you ready for me to come home, mentally and if so, how? One thing for certain is that you are the woman I have ever only truly loved, and I want us to have our connection like we are supposed to. LaShanna, you are ambitious, intelligent, a loyal friend and the most beautiful woman I have ever seen. I want you in my life forever, Sweetheart and I think about you constantly. Write me as soon as you are able because I miss you and know that above all else, I love you, LaShanna.

Love Lance

6-16-14

Song: Musiq Soulchild Don't Change

Baby Girl,

You know what Sweetheart, this is one of the many reasons why you are so special to me and why I love you so much. I appreciate the fact that you pay attention to details others so easily overlook and how you find ways to nurture me and learn more about me. Baby, I do understand how difficult it is to express your love and intimacy through our letters and being so far away. LaShanna, just as much as you want me down there, I want to be there with you and Tay just as bad. I think of nothing else but spending time with you, massaging your feet after a long day, holding you tight and listening to how you feel and what you think. Sweetheart, I want to be home with you to make sure the doors are locked at the end of the night or pick you up and carry you to our bedroom if you fall asleep in the living room. Being away from you like this kills me, Babe, but I know this is almost over, which means your husband will be home soon. I understand your reasons for encouraging me to be in good spirits and I want to have more than bitterness and regret to give our son. I like how you said, "You need to act like you have a little boy". I take pride in being a father and handling my responsibility as far as our little one is concerned. Don't worry though because Tay has a man in his life, the only one he will ever need. So as soon as possible, I want to be there to help raise him the right way and to show him what a man is supposed to be. To answer your question, yes LaShanna, you are the only woman I have ever truly loved and I realize it now more than ever. In my past relationships, I was caught up in the lust most of the time. But I should have known sooner that you were the one because I always thought about you, Babe. It was always you who I wanted to be with. No girl ever got as close to me or knew as much about me as you do. And as God as my witness, LaShanna, if at any moment you would've come to me wanting me, I would've left whatever situation I was in. I have loved you and been in love with you since the first time I heard your voice. Even your laugh makes my heart smile. On another note, I do want our union to be blessed and I believe you and I are meant to spend our lives with each other. So, I am going to work on praying again and having faith in God. Just to let you know, Sweetheart, although it may have been him allowing me to wake up each day. Babe, it has been you and my dreams about you that has gotten me through each day of this bid. I am feeling real crazy hearing about this almost accident. I am pissed, worried, and grateful at the same time. I cannot live without you or my Taylen, and the thought of something happening to either of you, I really can't deal with that. One thing for sure is that you and him being safe after that close call is the first thing I will thank God for tonight. Listen Beautiful, I need you to know that you are the love of my life, LaShanna. I am so very deeply in love with you and I am happy that we are continuing to move forward and building a life together. I truly apologize for being an asshole lately. I know that your position in my life is not only permanent, but irreplaceable, so I shouldn't act like that. I give you my promise never to send you a letter and not include a song to express my love and mood. So yes, I heard you, Babe. On another note, I was on some stressing shit back in April, My Love, and I stopped working out and gained 30 pounds, so I'm working on knocking it back down because I want you to think I'm sexy and I want to look good for you when I come home. You are right, I don't have a place in Jersey not right now, at least, but my home is in NC where my wife is. I never been to a hotel, but yes will need some where to go where I can fuck you all night without interruption. I cannot wait to feel your wet pussy on my tongue, Babe, for real. Anyway, yes love you lost a lot of weight and you are so gorgeous. Shit I was absolutely fine when you were thick, but for real, Shanna, you are so sexy. The curves in your lips are inviting, your eyes are the prettiest I ever saw, and I can't wait to stare into them and hold you in my arms. I like your pretty little hands, freshly manicure with your real nails. I love every single thing about you, LaShanna and it is a plus that you are the most beautiful woman my eyes have seen. Yeah Babe, you bad as hell. I would have liked to see you in your red and black outfit, and it's getting nice outside so I know you gone have them pretty ass feet out. Now do you see why I'm tripping about getting pictures of you and my little one. I miss you guys and I don't want to not be able to see you as much as possible even if its only pictures. Well, My Love, I will pause this moment in love with you for now so I can get started on answering those questions. Baby, I am glad that you are in my life and I truly love you with every fiber of my being, you are my everything. Please be careful down there and no matter what you may be doing throughout the day, know that your man is thinking about you, Babe. I love you so much, Sweetheart. Kiss Tay for me.

Love Lance

6-20-2014

Song: Chris Brown feat Jordan Sparks No Air

Mrs. Herring,

Baby I am so glad to get another letter from you today because I know the mail takes a while to come so I did not expect to hear from you until next week sometime. I do not want to get any further in this letter without telling you that you are so beautiful, LaShanna, and I thank you for the pictures you sent me, Sweetheart, I ain't stop smiling yet. It's not really something I can explain, but your smile does something to me. Baby, I am so lost in your eyes, I could stare at you all day long, and you are looking real delicious in your bathing suit. Damn, you are gorgeous in all your pictures, Babe. It kind of breaks my heart a little to see my little one getting so big. I really do love Taylen, Babe, and knowing that I am missing out on him growing doesn't feel good because in my mind at least, he is my son. I see we have one more thing in common besides cars, we are not too trusting of the ocean, but I do want him to learn how to swim. LaLa, I would give anything to have been home with you guys so we could have spent the holiday together. I could picture you trying to get me in that cold ass water and after saying no for the third time, you giving me that look and saying, "Babe, you really not gone go with me, not even halfway", and like the fool in love that I am, I'd go. Well, My Love, we have a lifetime of memories to create, as well as special moments to spend together, so let's look forward to that. This may seem random, but I love you, Baby. I love you more and more each passing moment that you are in my life. I wanted to make that clear because I get so caught up at times and neglect the fact that you have always been an important part of my life. So I thought it would be appropriate to let you know that I appreciate you, I adore you, and intend to spend the rest of our life together showing you how special you are, LaShanna. Aside from that, I really ain't digging your sister and her stupid ass comment seeing as through a woman raised me. So you had every right to go off on her for trying to downplay someone else, but I don't want you going back and forth like that. You know I ain't with too much talking anyway. I like how you explained what Facebook was. Baby, I ain't that deep in the cave. Listen Mama, everything is going to continue to work out for you and I, individually and collectively. You are strong, Baby, and I am seriously admiring how you still manage to work and raise our little one, on top of maintaining your relationship with me. I know it isn't easy but you really do a hell of a job Babe, so just hold it down a little longer. I will be there soon. I don't be wanting to admit shit like this because I don't want to sound corny, but you and Tay are all I think about all day every day, and I be missing you so intensely it drives me crazy at times but being in love with you is amazing. Nah, it's not sad that you sleep with my picture because I do something similar, but don't worry it's almost over. Yes of course, you are on my visiting list. You are my wife and you won't ever be removed. I do look forward to seeing you whenever it is possible but try and let me know in advance so I can get my shape up right and pay for our pictures, Babe. Also I have been working on praying since our last conversation. So I find you sexy in any style you choose. Oh yeah what you mean, I'm not pulling your hair?, We will see, you are my every fantasy. Babe, you really gone deny me. On another note, I have been okay Sweetheart, and I can do a little more to take care of myself, but I'm working on that. Anyway, LaLa when you write me again, I want you to send me your mom's house number and other numbers I can reach you at. I'm working on something and don't be rolling your eyes either, punk, just do it okay? Well, Mrs. Herring, this is all for now my Love, but I will be waiting to hear from my Baby Girl again soon. I want you to remember that even at times, I can't see you or touch you, I know you are there. So I want you to know I need you. Have a goodnight Baby, kiss my Taylen for me. I love you so much LaLa. Love Lance

P.S. Let me know how work is going, send the numbers and tell my mom-in-law I said hello.

6-23-14

Song: Jagged Edge I Gotta Be

LaShanna,

Hello beautiful, I got your letter in the mail a short while ago and did not want to delay in writing you a response. Babe, first things first, no matter what you tell me and what you withhold, I will still always worry about you and be concerned. You have to understand that you are the love of my life and the single most important thing in this world to me and since no one can care for you or protect you like me, I'll always worry in my absence. I really do not like hearing that you are having issues with your back, I never knew that much damage was caused in your accident, Babe. I'm not sure if you are able to do physical therapy or not but I want you to take it easy, Sweetheart. No heavy lifting, and when you wake up in the morning, I want you to stretch. See, this is the kind of stuff I should be at home for, to give you backrubs and massages. Don't worry so much about the firefighter physical, your ass won't be running up in anybody's burning house. What happened with the police exam? Have you changed your mind and are you open to other branches of law enforcement, court officer, probation, armored car service like Brinks? Also my Love, please don't focus on the negative, I do not believe your body will get worse and anyway I will be home sooner than later to help you with whatever. Thank you for sending more pictures of my little one. He looks so much like you, LaShanna, the same bright smile. By the way, I wear a size 12 or 12 ½ in Jordans, and since you keep Taylen fresh I want some too since my Christmas gift never happened and my birthday is coming, you know. Damn I really cannot believe how quickly these months are flying by. I'm not complaining though. Taylen knows the whole prayer huh? Its crazy cause when we were young, isn't that the same one we were taught? Hell no, do not let him grow no damn afro. When he gets a job, then he can decide to wear his hair how he wants. Anyway, Love, I really am happy and I'm also eagerly anticipate our time together, holding, hugging, and loving one another. I be kissing a picture of you before I go to sleep and as soon as I wake up in the morning. Oh yeah, I like how you laughed at me when my "I Love You" message was delivered. So what you think, I'm soft now? See, this is why I held back my feelings before. Things have been going okay lately, and honestly

I owe that to our progress because when we aren't right, Baby, I don't be giving a fuck about everything else. Other than your recent back pain, I hope everything is alright down there and you aren't stressed out, Babe. Well let me go for now cause I'm hungry as hell and I want to get this mailed before they pick up the mailbags. LaLa, I'm so tired of jail food. Anyway, Baby, I love you with all of my heart and will write again soon, Babe. Oh yeah, you can put our last name on your letter. I will still get my mail from you. Have a goodnight, Baby Girl, and know I am thinking about you and my Taylen constantly. Give him a kiss from me. I love you both so much LaShanna.

Love Lance

6-27-2014
Song: John Legend So High
      Janine & The Mixtape Hold Me


Baby Girl,

Good Evening my Love, I got another letter from you today and I swear I cannot remember the last time I was as happy as I have been lately. I did get the pictures and I love them Babe. You look very sexy in your Ninja Turtle tank top, plus those was my niggas when I was Taylen's age. Your personality is so unique and Baby, you have an unrivaled sense of style. Its seems like no matter what you wear, you always make any outfit look so damn good. Hearing you say that you aren't going anywhere, makes me feel good. Every now and then, men need a little reassurance and sense of security can only be strengthened by you, LaShanna. I know you are ready for me to be home already because I can think of nothing else but you and our family. There is no early release because my charge was "violent", but as of next summer, I will be eligible for the halfway house. Being that I am so close to coming home, I should've been going this summer, but since I got in so much trouble throughout my bid, I have 16pts which is too much when I need 4. I should be going to see parole in the next week or so. So this will set the tone for what is to come because they only remove 2pts a year for good behavior and I have only 2 years left so it's in their discretion to chop that 16 in half or be assholes and only take off 2. The reality is unless they just push me out, they can kiss my ass. I won't care about going when I only have 11 months left (it won't make sense). Anyway, don't worry too much Babe, they say the last leg of the race always seems longest, but we are almost there Baby…. almost. One thing I know is that I found the woman that I have always loved more than anyone or anything I have ever known. LaShanna, I swear I am going to be faithful, honest, and love you for the rest of my life. How is your back feeling though, Love? I know you said you were concerned about some back pains you were having the other week. You are so beautiful, Babe. Sorry, I look at your pictures as I write, I know that sounded random. Maybe a day or two ago something crossed my mind and began to pull me in a negative space, then I pulled out your photo album. I swear in this one picture, it was like you were really looking in my eyes and I heard your voice at the edge of my mind saying, 'baby let it go, things will work out'. It's crazy how we have known one another for fourteen years and things to me still feel so brand new. I would really like to have you in my arms this very moment so I could kiss you, Babe. My Queen, so full of life and so full of love. There is nothing I wouldn't do for you, Babe. There is no distance I wouldn't travel or risk I would not take, to see that smile. Who knew I could ever be in love like this and for so long? Anyway boo, I see you took my son to get his haircut. Yep he looks handsome like me, don't hate. I look forward to hugging him for the first time, the two of us cleaning the house before you get home and taking him to the park. Listen, Babe, even though the dynamics are a little different, you know how I love him and not only what he means to me, but what I will come to mean to him. So I want you to know I appreciate you allowing me to be part of our little one's life. Nothing will ever convince me that he is not mine because I will never treat him differently. Well, Beautiful, I must admit that things are okay. They are as best they can be under these conditions. LaShanna, I'm just grateful to be alive for the first time in my life and I can't wait to make things official between us and get married. I smile when I look back on our conversations about our wedding and family planning we use to have when were younger. You have given me some of the most memorable years I have lived and I am really happy that the dreams I use to have about us are coming true. Oh yeah, Babe, I asked for Ms. Lynn number because when the time comes I'm going to add it to my list so when the money get right, I'll be able to call you there at my expense. So even if you move again, I will still have that number in case you are there, and not at our house when I call one day. I see you mentioned something about a book so I will be looking out for it. You ain't even have to say that whatever my wife takes her time to send me, I am going to read it, bottom line. I love you so much, Baby. You do so much for me and I am becoming a better man because of you, Mrs. Herring. Make sure you let me know in your next letter how you are feeling, Sweetheart, and how things at work have been going. You going to teach me how to swim huh, well let me just let you know, there is only one and only one ocean I want to swim in and that's yours, Babe. Okay, let me stop being fresh, listen little mama. I want to get this letter mailed to you so I will pause this moment infinitely in love with you until I hear from you again. LaShanna, I love you with all my heart Baby, and you will be on my mind and in my heart until I hear from you. Please be careful down there, Babe. You know how I am about you. Have a goodnight Baby Girl and kiss my Taylen for me. I love you Sweetheart.

Love Mr. Herring

P.S. I love the pictures you always tease my unquenchable thirst for you. By the way, Who the hell is Ray? I Love You Sexy

6-29-2014

Song: Tank You're My Star

LaShanna,

In these moments of clarity I am pulled deeper in love with you and I appreciate the woman you are. You have a way of making me hate the world a little less so that I have room to love you that much more. After a busy ass Saturday I came back and was surprised by another letter from my wife. After reading it, I see one of your letters must have come earlier than another because now I'm getting the one explaining who Raymond is and what he has to do with my Baby. When I read it, my jealousy began to react. I mean let's keep it 100, it ain't no secret about the way I cherish you, but it's like you kind of seeing through the nigga. Now Babe, before I give my opinion on the situation, let me be clear that if you consider him a friend, I won't intrude but as a man and as your husband, I'm telling you he is full of shit and let me explain. For starters if he was genuinely your friend, you would've been hearing from him instead of not having spoken since 2008. Now Babe, ain't no nigga in this day and age proposing to no woman because they have a child together. The bottom line is he is either getting cold feet or he just ain't feeling homegirl like he convinced her he

146

was and is looking for a way out. This is where you come in. Now all of a sudden, he plants a seed, putting it in your mind that he has always had some feeling for you, BULLSHIT. Baby, he is manipulating his vulnerability to gain sympathy from you, so when things finally go downhill with him and homegirl, he can fall back on you. Hence the whole 'I shoulda, woulda, coulda with you'. I think you should not entertain this nigga because not only does he not see you as the friend you think he does. He thinks you are naïve enough to have your emotions as a woman toyed with unnoticed. Let me also make clear, LaShanna, if you have male friends, I am very uncomfortable with you spending time alone with a man. If it is a group setting, that's different. But all that one-on-one shit is out. I still never let go the situation with that nigga that kissed you because he thought your friendship was more than that. I still wanna smack his head off his fucking shoulders for that shit. Anyway, Sweetheart, I do appreciate that you respect me enough to let me know what happened. For real, Baby, thank you for being honest. Oh yeah Babe, don't allow your judgement to be clouded by peoples opinion of your loyalty. You owe your loyalty to your family and me, your husband. You had me bugging over my answers to those questions I sent you. Nah boo, I wasn't playing safe, I was honest. Your assessment about me wanting to stay in bed all day and make love to you is accurate. I can't front, Babe. I will not try to get you pregnant immediately, but it's tempting. I do want you and I want to have our time together. Just to let you know, Baby Girl, no matter what may come, I am going to stay by your side and I will be faithful to you LaLa. I don't want nobody else. I will stop telling you about eating you out. I never knew you felt like that, but you know I'm not with that talking stuff anyway. I will be mindful of that because I don't want to turn you off in anyway and I damn sure don't want to remind you of anybody. You know I hate being compared to niggas. It is flattering that you thought I would've had more sexual partners, but nah Babe, not many women can appreciate the sexiness of a 400lb man. One thing I do know is that I want you to be my last first kiss, and you will definitely be the last woman I make love to for the first time. Wait hold the fuck up…did you say your gay friend is having problems with his boyfriend? lol. I mean, damn what could they possibly argue about, who gone wear the wig this time? lol. Okay let me stop cause that's not nice. Baby, please don't be having them around my little one because I don't want him having that type of influence. I mean I have no problem that he's gay. I just don't want him around my Tay too much. On another note, I am very curious about this sign that God sent you about us, but I will wait until I get home so you can tell me so I hope you don't forget. I know one damn thing, I hope I'm not going to want to hurt anyone for hurting you. You are all I have,

Babe, you know I hate it when you are hurt or you aren't safe. I know there will be times when you have doubts about things but we are going to make it, LaShanna, I promise you, Baby. And in the midst of making it is where we will enjoy our happiness. Watch, you'll see. You are an excellent mother. You do everything you can with what you have and I will be home soon to balance out what seems like a burden. But you are doing a hell of a job, LaLa. These are the kinds of things that make you perfect in my eyes. Now about my mom's, even though you scared of her, she actually does like you, Babe, you have no idea. You will see for yourself though. I'm mad I won't be able to get my birthday gift, but when I get there, I want you to give it to me over and over for all of the birthdays I missed (wink). I'd love hearing you scream because I'll know I'm doing my job… And you are on my list, Babe. I had to change the address, but I may have put the wrong birthday. I know you're a week after me. Damn I have to catch my breath, I just had one of those moments and I realize how deep in love with you I am. Baby, you got me wrapped around all ten of your pretty fingers and toes. By the way, I have a question, Babe. When I am making love to you from the missionary position, if I took one of your feet off my chest and sucked your toes, would it turn you off. Hell no I never did that with another woman EVER, but I want to do it to you, Babe and only you. Anyway Sunshine, oh I almost forgot to tell you I had a dream about you last night and I could not fall back asleep because it felt so real. My thoughts about you kept racing. The only thing I remember was that I made some hot chocolate and after you said you didn't want none, I caught you in our dining room with mine. So I'm like nah, give me my cup, then you said, you ain't like it, then you gone say to me you only like when I make it lol sounds exactly like something you would do. Then you was writing something on our refrigerator and you turned around and leaned against me and I gave you a kiss. It's crazy Babe, I mean I could really feel my arms around your waist, but I woke up after that. Well my Love, this is all for now, but I like the way we are communicating and thank you for taking your time to write me like you've been. Baby, you are spoiling me. If you aren't careful, I may get used to it. So let me go for now, my Queen, but I end this letter loving you more than anything in this world. I thank God that I have you because I believe I found love at its best and with you, it will be forever this time. LaShanna, I love you, Sweetheart, be safe down there. I don't want to hurt anyone. Have a good evening my Love, I pray you are reading these words during the beautiful sunset I wrote them to. I love you so much, Mrs. Herring, kiss my little one for me.

Love your husband, Mr. Herring

6-30-2014

Song: Usher #1 Fan

Baby,

Good Evening, my Sexy, today was such a long busy ass day for me, and just when I thought I was too exhausted to do anything else, I got a letter from my Queen. It felt so good to see the envelope and see LaShanna Herring. Damn Babe you sure know how to make a man feel good for the first time in years. I woke up and got to my knees to thank God for the day, among other things. I still can't believe it myself. Now getting to your letter, you know you can't beat me, so what were you saying, you gone fuck who up, how? What I meant when I said I would be home sooner than later, I was talking about the possibility of making it to the halfway house but, also indicating that whether I did or not won't matter because I am so close to coming home anyway. Sweetheart, I know some days are longer than others and I know you want me at home already, but I'm coming Babe. Look at it this way, in January I'll have what 18 months to go, no more years to count, Babe. And no, I cannot have any Jordans in here. I meant for you to get them so they will be there when I come home. I want me coming home to feel like a reality to you instead of just part of our conversations, so I thought I should be getting things together for when I come down there. By the way, we need to have a serious talk about that because I want to make sure you are ready, Babe. Plus you know it won't be easy finding a job being an ex-felon with no degree, so I'm going to need your support. Baby, I love you I mean truly inside and out, so I want to add to your life not take away. It is one thing to talk about me moving in, and another for me to actually be there. I don't want you to get tired of me or feel like I'm smothering you and intruding on your space. So let me know how you feel about this, my Love, because if the chance arises that I can transfer my parole there instead of having it up here, and still being away from you for 3-5 more years, I want to know how you feel about it and be honest. About this Michael Kors backpack, I can't exactly look that up, LaLa, but how much is it? Also, even though you say your back only hurts on and off, I don't like that you are hurting period and I'm mad I can't make it better. I really ain't too thrilled about you going anywhere to do laundry. We definitely will have our own washer and dryer. Babe, you never told me what the cost of living is down there either. I mean where are we going to live? You know married couples get better house loans, just saying, Babe. Anyway Sunshine, please don't allow things to get you down because you really are doing such a good job, Baby. I need you to stay strong for me the way you always have because things are going to get better. On

top of that, I am here for you, Baby. We can get through anything and we will together. Well, Big Head, let me go for now so you can get this as soon as possible. Baby I miss you, I miss you every second, minute, and hour of everyday. As soon as the money get right, I got you Babe, and this time I don't wanna hear that "you don't have to" nonsense. You and Taylen are my number one priority.It is my job to provide for my family, regardless of my situation. Mrs. Herring, I love you. Sweetheart, please kiss Taylen for me. I will speak to you soon, Beautiful. Sweet dreams my Love.
Love Lance


7-1-2014

Song: Jeffrey Osbourne Love Ballad

LaShanna,

There is something about loving you, it soothes my soul, it warms my veins when my heart is cold. Something about loving you, reminds me of our younger days, memories I will reminisce on and relive when we are old in age. There is something about loving you that ignites my hope, keeping me anchored and in love with you ever since the first time we spoke. Through each season of our union, I will remain loyal and true. This life means nothing without your presence or that something there is about loving you.

Love Always Lance

I woke up and panicked because you were in my dream and I couldn't remember it. But these words were on my heart and I wanted to share them with you. Baby, I love you…Enjoy the holiday.

7-3-2014

Song:  Faith Evans I Love You
        Whitney Houston I Look To You

Mrs. Herring,

Good Morning, Sweetheart, I want to begin this letter by first saying that I Love You so much and that I am yours.

I will always be yours. Something amazing happened to me, it confirmed that I am moving in the right direction and that we were made for one another Babe. I was about to beat the shit out this nigga over some dumb shit and he did all the right things that would have given me every right. So I get the police to open the nigga cell door and I stepped inside, as soon as I felt my adrenaline spike, which is usually when I swing. Baby, I felt a hand in the middle of my chest. I felt a palm and five fingers kind of push me back just lightly and a voice said, "Lance, Don't". In that split second, I looked down because the way I was touched could only have come from someone shorter than me, but the shit that really has me bugging is that those words were your voice.

So I calmed down, but I did check the nigga and his response was way different than it was when he was popping shit from behind the door. That whole thing really has me trippin, Babe, because I have never experienced anything like that. So I've been staring at one of my favorite pictures of you. They're all my favorite, but looking into your eyes, it feels so real, my Love, like you are actually here with me. Then thinking about you giving me the business about how I do have a little one to answer to for my actions and the way I conduct myself put things in perspective for me. LaLa, I cannot imagine my life without you or without Taylen, and Baby, I promise to do whatever I must to not only make it home to you two, but to also provide a comfortable living when I get there. Baby, you have always been in my life, especially doing the most pivoted points and that means a lot to me. So I really want to be the man to spend the rest of my life making it up to you, making you feel appreciated as a loving mother, devoted friend, and an amazing wife. I almost forgot to mention that my book came yesterday, and yes I read it immediately, thank you Baby. It is the little things like that, let me know how much you care and I intend to read that book once every month so it all sinks in. I really like Chapter 4 because it discusses having a good woman in your life, and I have the greatest woman any man could wish to have in mine. LaShanna, if I had to describe what a perfect woman was, it still wouldn't measure up to the strong and very beautiful black woman you are. I have been watching the news and saw some hurricane warning down there, so I hope you and our family are doing okay and aren't being negatively affected by it. Also little Mama, I need to hear your voice so I will be giving you a call sometime next week because I be missing you, Baby. Anyway, the Fourth of July is tomorrow and if the weather is okay, I know you're going to be at somebody's cookout. I hope you have fun and are being safe. Shit if I had to do 10 years for something I didn't do, I definitely have no qualms about doing more if anyone hurts or disrespects you, Sweetheart. So I will pause this moment in love with you for now, Babe. But you remain in my heart and in the center of my thoughts. I love you, punk, even though you can't fight. You'll always be my Queen. Enjoy the rest of your day, Beautiful. I will speak to you soon. Kiss Taylen for me, let him know he is loved.

Love Only, Yours Truly Mr. Herring

P.S. LaShanna, you are a dream come true…smile for me Baby, I love you.

7-6-2014

Song: Algebra Blessett Nothing But You

Baby,

I am still kind of speechless. I can't believe your ass would play a trick on me like that. I can't even really describe what I was feeling or thinking as I read those words. It was like my whole body got numb and I couldn't breathe, and this was before the pain of my injured pride and hurt feelings set in. Sweetheart, I have never felt so scared or experienced such a sense of loss, that hurt me more than when I got sentenced for real, Boo. I felt like I was losing my life. I'm not upset with you cause that was one hell of a prank. You better believe I'm gonna get that ass back for that one, watch? I can appreciate it though because you showed me how deeply invested in our relationship I really am. LaLa, you have no idea my love of how much I need you in my life. Babe, you gave me a sobering glimpse of how things would be if I ever lost you. I don't ever intend for that to happen neither because I can't live without my Queen. I am flattered by some of the ways you expressed feeling about me and as promised, I will not let you or our little one down. Please don't ever joke like that again. You still got my hands shaking, but goddamn if you don't make being in love with you feel so fucking good, it's like I am addicted to you. You had me itching to find out this nigga name and where he was from. Trust, I was gonna get his ass. You got that one though, Baby Girl. I ain't trippin, but I'm gone get you for that. Anyway, Beautiful, Happy July to as well. Everything has been going smoothly. It's like everything slowly, but surely falling into place. You have me a bit more optimistic about things these days and honestly, I'm just getting prepared to come home and being with you and our family. I still have been making it a priority to pray at least once a day which is usually in the morning before I go to work. I am learning to appreciate things I would normally have taken for granted, and more than anything I be thanking God for blessing me with a very special woman, who I love and cherish unconditionally (you,

Baby). Now getting to your other letter, Babe, I am relieved to hear that your back is feeling okay now and I'll be home eventually to massage you when it hurts. Wherever it hurts. I know you need me to be there especially when the stress becomes overwhelming and I will be, Sweetheart. Just hold on for me a little longer. I be laying here daydreaming about cradling you in my arms, holding you tight, and giving you the assurance that you and Taylen are safe and that I will always be there. I had no clue you were out of work that long, but I do agree with you needing a break. Being a mom and wife is a full-time job. Okay, let us discuss you potentially moving back up here because I have mixed feelings. Listen, Sunshine, there is nothing that would make me happier than having you closer to me because when I say I want to come home to you, I mean that. I want to turn the key in our door and smell your scent as soon as I cross the threshold, I want to lay with you every single night and wake up to you next to me every morning, Baby. I want those things now instead of having to wait, but I also want what's in you and my sons best interest. You moved to N.C for a reason and down there, at least I know we can get our money's worth as far as affordable living and things are quiet. I never intended to live out my days up here in the tri-state area so to have you move up here just to have us move out of state again seems unfair to you. I want Taylen to have his own backyard, as well as quality education. I do not want to raise our family in Jersey City or Newark. I want us to be in a safe neighborhood where I don't have to carry a gun like I did. Plus, I really don't want to have to put Alvin in the ground. I am concerned that if you and Tay become more accessible to him and he is going to do or say something stupid, and I'm gone finish his ass. At the same time, LaLa, I do want you close, Babe. I can't even lie about that but let me know your thoughts and feelings about coming back. I mean if it's just to be with me, I am still working on the details of moving my parole where you are. However, if you want to move up here for other reasons, that is a different matter. But like I said, let's talk about it some more and take it from there babe. I miss you a lot though, big head. I can't wait to hear your voice this week. Yes, I am feening for you so what? Don't think I overlooked the fact that you were sitting in that hot ass car in front of the post office to write me this letter. LaShanna, I love and really appreciate you so much. Things like this is what makes you so special to me Babe. I love you with all my heart and soul. Well Mrs. Herring, I'm gone pause this moment in time and that much more in love with you because I want you to get this soon. LaLa, you are everything I want and everything I need. I won't ever let you go, Babe. In the meantime, please kiss my Taylen for me and tell him I love him. Be careful down there too. Love is Love Baby Girl…and mines is forever. I Love You.

Love Eternally,
Your Husband, Mr. Herring

P.S. you said you would leave me if I ever lied, cheated, or stopped being in love with you. But on the survey you said if I cheated, we had to talk. LaShanna, you are the best thing that has ever happened to me and I will NEVER do any of that. I could never again live without you Babe, you make me feel complete.

7-8-2014

Song: Tank Next Breath

LaShanna,

You smell so good baby, every time I get another letter from you, I hold it close and inhale you into my senses. I couldn't take my 1 o'clock nap today because I couldn't stop thinking about my Queen long enough to quiet my thoughts. I am very glad to hear from you again, Love. And you are right, as soon as I mail you one letter another one comes, but I'm loving it, Boo. Now let's see, oh yeah, Babe, you ain't have to worry about me being upset with the whole Raymond conversation. Yes, I was jealous because I hate the thought of another man looking at you in the ways I see you. However, I'm more insulted than anything that a nigga would think my wife isn't intelligent enough to see through bullshit like them other bitches out there. You are far from ordinary Babe, and I hate for you to be compared to other females because you are one of one, none before and none to come. I had to laugh about what you saying about your uncle. Only because of course, you gone love him regardless, he is family. I understand what you are saying though and I am going to be mindful of my comments because I realize you don't like how I criticize myself at times. I mean I was always satisfied with me, it's just that I just wanted to be attractive in your eyes, Baby. Your opinion of who I am and how I look is the only one that matters. I guess I look back to when we were kids and remembering some comments you made about certain men on T.V. And shit like that, and since none of them looked like me, I never felt like I was your type or that you found me sexy. For the record, I love how your body looks and can't wait to touch how it feels. LaShanna, no matter how much weight you lose or put on, you will always be the most beautiful woman these eyes have seen. I'm glad that I have your support and also that I can have confidence in knowing your love for me is undying and unconditional as mine will always be for you. No disrespect to your gay buddies, but I am relieved that my little one has not had that influence. Damn, I really wanna be home and help raise our son. I see where you said that there are a lot of things you want to tell me but face-to- face, I just hope you don't forget. You know how you do. Speaking of my mother, I forgot to mention to you in my last letter how I sat her down. First, on the phone and then on the visit and explained to her how deeply in love with you I was as well as my reasons for feeling that way. Check you out, you nervous already, but you know my mother is understanding and very down-to-earth so of course, we have her support, Baby. LaShanna, you not only are beyond good enough for me, Baby Girl, you are everything I could have wished to find in a woman. I was so broken, Babe, because of all of the shit that I've lived through and you pulled me out the gutter and showed me how real love felt. Baby, you are so much more than you have given yourself credit for. You taught me that real love is special and only occurs once in a lifetime. You have shown me that love is also about redirecting your life and decisions. More importantly you nurture me mentally and spiritually, Babe. So I can't do anything short of dedicating my life to you. Anything less is unacceptable. Now about your b-day, I never forgot. I just absent mindedly wrote the date on the slip, kind of like how I did with my letter last week. But okay, I'll take my punishment. But my day for no sex will be today. You just make sure you take your punishment like a big girl when I get home. On another note, my Love, I asked about your toes because I want to show you that there is really nothing I won't do to make your pussy quiver. Plus that is a very intimate thing to do but I got you Babe. After all, you did say as long as it feels good right? As far as my Taylen goes, I remember being his age and fighting because the teachers don't do they job so I agree that he needs to defend himself, but that spitting stuff, nah we don't play that. Let's be clear, I just want him to box, so he'll have the skill and so he'll be active.

I'll teach him how to fight so I'm definitely not worried about them country ass crumb snatchers down there. Shit we from the old school. Okay Princess, I am coming to the end of your letter and reading the quotes that you left for me and I am somewhat speechless, as well as humbled. It is definitely true that I love you, Baby because you have always been in my prayers since we were younger and that is a beautiful thing to reflect on. LaShanna, I also want my marriage, family, home, and future to be built with you. Baby, I have wanted you all of my life and you can trust my words are more than promises. I can never love another woman nor do I desire to be with another woman that isn't YOU. Through God's grace, I will see my intentions with you and Taylen fulfilled. I have always believed in my heart that you were meant for me and honestly in comparison to my love for you, none else exists. Babe, we have both been through a lot, but I won't take any paths on this journey that don't lead to you. We will get where we need to and endure every storm along the way together, Babe, me, and you. I have never been to heavy on religion, but I am learning and getting there slowly, and as long as I have my wife continuing to encourage me and nourish me the way you have, I can continue to be open and receive God's blessing. Baby Girl, I believe with all of my heart that you are my greatest blessing and you are the woman I need and can't live without. So thank you for your patience, Sweetheart. I appreciate your effort to groom me and make me a better man. I will continue to pray for our marriage and friendship to be a healthy and happy one. I will always pray for the safety of you and our little one, I'll lose my mind without you and Tay. Well, Pretty Lady, I want you to know that your husband loves you so much. In the meantime, Babe, give Taylen my kiss and tell him I love him, tell him constantly. Be careful down there, Sweetheart and have a goodnight sleep Babe. I love you, Mrs. Herring…See you later, Sexy.

Love Always Mr. Herring

P.S. All of me loves all of you (never forget Baby cause I won't let you).

7-10-2014
Song: Drake Too Much

Ms. Lady,

First off, let me say I was glad to speak to you yesterday and you sounded nervous as hell, but were doing a decent job of covering up. Then by time you began to sound comfortable, the call was ending. Now today, I am getting a letter you wrote to me on the 4th of July. I am a bit confused about some of what you asked me and even more so curious about why you asked none of this during our call? As far as me being ready to change my environment goes, I always intended to relocate once this was over so I would've left the tri-state area whether I was with you or not. About when I wanted to get married, I wanted to when I thought I found the right one that wasn't going to put me through any bullshit, someone who was going to make me their number one priority, and most of all when I could afford. Due to this letter from you, I am beginning to second guess myself since it seems you have some doubts about me. Also, I'm not sure what you mean about having other stuff on my mind, but you know I've been gone since 08' and will have served 8 ½ years. You also know I left at 19 so I wasn't afforded the chance to explore my life and have 'me' time or any of that. Which you need to take into consideration, but I'll let you explain to me what that means so I don't answer what isn't being asked. I'm unclear why any of this is being said because if my intentions wasn't right, I wouldn't mess with you. There are plenty of females I could've ran whatever game on with little or no effort on my part, who could be closer in distance with none of the complications. So again, I'm unclear on why it seems like you questioning my intent. I am offended and obviously aggravated now. I'm sure you know by my writing. I'm gone stop here and wait on some explanation from you cause this caught me way off guard.

Love Lance

P.S.. why you keep saying shit like "in case something happens"? this is the third time, LaShanna. Is something happening I need to know and where you get this lazy drunk bum shit from? I hate liquor and I always kept a job.

7-11-2014

Song: Candice Glover Passenger

Baby,

You aren't going to like the other letter I sent you and I know that, but I tried as best as I know how to express how I felt without wanting to hurt your feelings. I have been up since 3am this morning, thinking about it and I'm just confused about why you would ask me that. It made me feel like not only were you having second thoughts about me, but that I wasn't good enough for you or Taylen because of how you said things. I can understand you wanting him to be raised in a healthy environment, but sometimes you say shit like I have to meet his standards, like you don't know me and I'm some nigga you just met. I'm not criticizing your parenting methods, but it seems like you are trying to shield him from a few realities that he will face one day on his own. So saying things like you don't want him to see me like this or that is offensive like I am not entitled to be human. I have been in love with you too long for you to EVER question whether I am really ready for a life with you. Especially because if you were anyone else, our communication would have ended the second you told me you were pregnant. Baby, I am the one who after being gone so long did not think twice before deciding to come home and take on a responsibility like that, on top of the fact, relocating to do so. No nigga my age who served the time I'm serving, would even consider something like this, and just so you know, having time to "live my life" or "do me" never crossed my mind because you are my life, you and Taylen. So I deserve a little more respect than this. I believe a marriage is two people deciding they are going to be together and stay together regardless of what happens and I want to marry you, LaShanna. I would've married you already if not for the fact that I am in here. So I hope this answers your question about how soon I want to get married. I want to marry you now, Baby. I do what I've done in the streets and I keep that shit away from my family. I have been this one person all my life and will never change, but you as my best friend and as my wife should have the confidence in me to know I would never intentionally expose my son to something wrong, my son, my Taylen (Fuck Alvin). So be honest,

Sweetheart, please if you are changing your mind about me or us, let me know so I don't continue to plan for things that may not happen. Anyway, I was okay with the idea of the Candlewood place, but I don't like that its only one floor and pets are conditional because I'm getting a dog, that's non-negotiable. I mean those are ranch style houses, I'm a king and need a basement or at least 2 levels, but I do like the amenities Babe. Look Sweetheart, I don't wanna argue about this. I just want you to be straight up about how you feel instead of spoon- feeding me. Now when you said I have to let you in a little more what do you mean? I will be waiting on your response, but in the meantime I do love you, Baby, and I want you to tell me what I have to do to show you that you are all I want. If you think I'm bullshitting, we can go get married the first week I'm home, Babe. Yea you scared now. I love you, Mrs. Herring.

Love Lance

P.S. I want you to be sure you can be the woman I need in my life because I was sure 14 years ago.

7-18-2014
Song: Tupac Keep your Head Up

Sweetheart,

I got two letters from you today and one of them is very wrinkled like you were crying on the paper and it makes me feel like shit. Before anything else, I need to address my response to your last because clearly you misinterpret a few things the same as I did. My mentioning other females was to basically explain to you that I would waste time with someone else before I ever hold false intentions to build a life with you. Maybe it was the wrong …no, it was the wrong analogy to use and I apologize for coming off like I was being accusatory or for making it appear that you were an option. Baby, you and Taylen are my life, LaShanna, and I would never leave you for anyone or anything under any circumstances, so don't talk about gladly letting me go anywhere. The rest of my life is built around you and my little one, so how can I survive without you. Babe, I was only making inquiries and trying to find out what made you pose the questions that you did. And after I got the next letter from you about some of the shit Alvin put you through, answered those questions for me. But my other letter was already sent. Yes my Love, you are my wife and I love you, Shanna.

Trust me, I know your actions speak louder than words, Babe. I'm not doubting you. Baby, when it's all said and done, I do have your back and you have my word that I will be more mindful of things I could say that may make you feel otherwise. So you ask me am I scared to be "someone's" husband and I'm going to be honest, I am scared to be "someone's", but not yours. Being with you is the only thing in my life that ever-made complete sense. So I would never be someone else's that isn't LaShanna. Now to answer your other question, yes I really want to get married because if it was possible and you were open to it, I would've married you already, Babe. You talking about getting a dress and I was talking about going to the courthouse asap. Nah, seriously though, Sweetheart, weddings cost money. So if you would rather have a nice wedding, we are going to have to save and it would have to wait a little longer than my first week home. Listen Mama, you let me know what you want and how you want it because I want our wedding to be special and I won't cheat you out of our fairytale ending. I told you, you are my Princess. On to a serious subject now, this whole shit with Alvin is really pissing me off. If he feels like its fuck you and my son and actually had the nerve to say that bullshit then maybe you should consider asking him to sign over his rights. That way he don't have to worry about either one of you or I will take it from there. Explain to me what Taylen's expenses are as far as school so I can see what can be done about it. Damn Baby, I blew through $1000 dollars a few months ago and I wish you would've allowed me back then to share in my son's financial obligations because he would've been taken care of. Please do not worry so much Babe. I know shit is getting tough and you can't see a way out right now, but things will work out, Sweetheart. You already know as soon as I get my hands on it, I'm sending you half, do not argue with me about this cause it's not up for discussion. Close your eyes for me and take a deep breath, Baby, we are going to get through this, I promise. I don't know why your mom doesn't wanna help, but we aren't going to dwell on it, Babe. Like I said, just explain the school payments to me and I'll do my best to send you what I have when I can. This kills me, Babe, that the two most important people in the world really need me, and I can't be there physically like I want to. Shanna, I know you are hurting, but never feel bad about discussing anything with me about you or our little one. I also don't like these eerie feelings you have been having, and it was worrying me because I thought someone was threatening or harassing my wife, cause I'm not having that shit. I think you are dealing with so much and you feel like you don't have anyone who understands or truly cares. But you do, Babe, because I am here and I care. Thank you for doing the things you do that engage me in the outside world and that keep me encouraged and take my mind out of this place, Baby. Yes, getting on with my life will be different after this. It will be much better because I will be able to finally be with the one I have waited my whole life for and that's you, LaShanna. No, it's not and never will be a win to lose with you, Baby. I had to lose everyone and everything in my life to win you. God had to make room in my life for the greatest blessing he could ever give me. Boo I apologize again for saying what I said and the way I said it because I don't want to add to your headaches or argue with you. I love you, Babe, let me go so I can start on your next letter.

Love Always, Your Husband, Mr. Herring

P.S.. I have to take everything you say to heart because what you say matters to me, Baby, and Ima get my act right because I need you and never wanna lose you Baby Girl.

7-18-2014

Song: Usher Love You Gently

Baby Girl,

Hello again, Sweetheart I had to take a brief break to close my eyes and pray for my family and to ask God to help you and I find a way through this bump in our road. I love the way you sing, Babe, I remember years ago when you accidently left me a voicemail with you singing. I saved that message until my phone service got cut off, I never told you that. However, I definitely would have liked to have been home so I could carry you from our bathroom to our bedroom after your shower, Babe. Just by the sweet smell after your letter, I can only imagine how your body smells after you take a shower. It's good to know you will let me lotion your body, Babe, and yes, you know me so well because I would definitely sneak a taste of your sweetness. Damn, you are right! Let us stop because thinking about you polishing my trophy is starting me up, plus my dick is a little sore from earlier. I had a dream about you, Babe, and I couldn't help myself. Shanna, each and every letter I write to you and every word I say is the truth of how I feel for you, Babe. I always felt like our spirits were linked so it's like DeJa'Vu hearing you say that. I love you so much, Babe. I believe that if reincarnation was real, my soul would always seek yours out in each life. Can't you see that I belong to you, Babe? You complete me, Mrs. Herring. I never knew I could ever be so in love, but it definitely isn't hard to see why. I have faith in us and have absolutely no doubt that we will become Mr. and Mrs. Because in my heart, we already are. Anyway, Beautiful, I will speak to the parole liaison this week and see how I can go about making this move happen because I hate being this far away from you, Baby. You are right, there is a lot of bullshit going on up here. And I always felt like if I stayed, I would end up back in here or in someone's cemetery. So I really wanna move. I need you to do something for me. Please don't ever refer to yourself as a bitch because you are a Queen, Baby. I know you need me there with you and I am going to be there with you as soon as possible. You'll see, Boo, just hold on for me a little longer. I always think from time to time why we never ended up together as we got older. But at least now, we recognize what real love is, Babe. The fact that you and I always seemed to find our way back to one another over the years, speaks volumes. Nothing can convince me that you weren't made for me, Shanna nor I for you. So now that you came back in my life, I'm never letting you go because I can't be happy without you and my Taylen, I believe that with every fiber of my being.

You can give me your heart, Babe, I really love you so much and I know you are here for me. I never knew they had drive-in movies, I only seen that kind of stuff on TV (Poetic Justice). I'm feeling some type of way that I missed out on that, I need to be with my family. We are going to have the opportunity to do family time together, so you should not be feeling like we won't get the chance. Baby just hold on I'm coming home. I want to take him to the zoo and for us to go horseback riding and things like that. I'll never be too gangster to spend quality time with our family. Don't be scared, my Love, our time is coming. And I cannot wait, Babe, seeing your beautiful face and pretty smile every day and hearing Taylen laugh. You know what's crazy? I worry sometime about him waking up needing to go potty in the middle of the night and if there is a night light in the bathroom. I love you two so much Babe, ya'll really consume all my thoughts because when I'm not thinking about him, I'm thinking about you, Gorgeous...Constantly, Babe. I be wanting to make Taylen cereal in the mornings and practice his numbers and letters with him. I want to teach my son how to tie his shoes and things like that. I am going to be there for you when you are having a bad day to help you undress and bring you chilled wine and fruit while you take your bath and tell me about it. Shanna, I'm here now, but I will be there then to pull you on my lap and hug you close when the world is getting on your nerves. You are going to know that someone loves you and will protect you at all times, Baby, physically, emotionally, and mentally. My mother did look surprised because of the way I broke shit down to her about what I loved about you and why I was in love with you, and she was very supportive. But yeah, Little Mama, you definitely put some kind of spell on me, but I never want it to wear off. I love you, Baby Girl. Oh and yes that was what my random question was about. So thanks for answering, but I ain't need you to tell me you did it before "plenty of times". I hate knowing someone else shared such a priceless moment with you and was eating my cake in the process. But no when I do it, you won't be tasting yourself because I'm swallowing everything, and you will have a taste because I'll use caramel syrup and whip cream from the bottom of your ass to the top of your clitoris. I can show you better. Okay, my Heart, let me pause this moment in time and still falling deeper and deeper in love with you. Your handwriting is never sloppy, so don't worry about it. But Baby, I do appreciate you staying up late to finish writing me. It just made my heart skip when you said Tay puts me in his prayers. I hope he knows how much I care for him because I love him so much. I wrote him a letter back in January that I wanted you to give him when he got older but forgot where I put it, I'll find it. Shanna, I love you with all my heart, Pumpkin, for real and you make me so happy, Baby. Please be careful down there, Sweetheart, and don't forget, I am here for you. We are in this eternally and can get through anything together. Have a goodnight sleep, my Queen, and kiss my Taylen for me, I love you both so so much. Love Lance

P.S. I made no mistakes, the stamps were for you in case you were running low. I Love You, Baby.

7-21-2014

Songs: Fantasia Only One You
        Joe I Wanna Know

My Love,

Baby, you smell so good. I smelled your letter mad times and I still cannot seem to get enough of your scent. It is so sweet I can almost taste you. Of course I was more than excited to hear from my Baby. And yeah, I be counting the days. I be feenin huh. Well what can I say? Sweetheart, your love is a powerful drug. I am relieved to hear that you are in better spirits now because I don't like when you be feeling like the world is crashing down on you Baby. But I want you to remember in your most stressful moments that your husband is here for you, Babe. I could say it a million times, but Shanna, you will never really know how special or how important you are to me Little Mama (I Love You). I admire your creativity with your acronym for T.R.U.E L.O.V.E. I believe it is unique to our relationship and its exactly what I have always wanted. Babe, I am also grateful to God for allowing me to experience it with the only woman I have ever truly wanted it with. Check you out, funny prison stories. Babe, this ain't the kind of spot where funny shit happens in here. I mean I thought it was hilarious when some nigga got hot water tossed on his ass. He was screaming like a bitch and running around. The funny shit to me was the trail of steam that was coming from his head as he ran. I will compromise with you about your shows. lol I be watching 'Teen Mom' and 'Love and Hip Hop' lmao. I already know my 'Bad Girls Club' watching will be over when I get there. So I mind as well stop while I'm here. I do like HGTV (some show with Egypt), but lately I've been into this show called 'Married at First Sight'. It's on FYI channel only because it reminds me of the amazing love we share. Now about my Taylen, I am so proud that he has the desire to learn especially at his age. Shanna, I want to be home with him so bad. I'm jealous that I am missing these years of his life, Babe. All I can do is use this as motivation to never let this happen again because being away from you two is not easy, my Love. Since he is always done with the series you brought for him, I will add sending my little man more books to my list of things to do. This is actually a coincidence because I ordered a catalog the other week and was going through a selection appropriate for his age that I think he may like. I also found that letter I told you I wrote for him a while back. Shit it took me two days, but I finally found it. The only thing is I can't remember everything I wrote and I stapled it closed so you wouldn't read it (Nosey). Anyway, Love, I see you are going to the gym and I am ok with it as long as you don't do anything to hurt yourself, Babe, but remember that my love and desire for you is unconditional, so I'm happy with how you look at all times. But please don't get all boney. Oh yeah, before I forget, Boo, I do like the price of the house you was telling me about, I don't know how I'll be able to afford my half because I don't want you to have to pay for everything. I mean I eventually would like for us to purchase a home together, Babe, and we gotta pay for water at that one (smh). I do plan on us having a dishwasher so that is a concern of mine. I think an apartment would be better choice financially until we can afford a house. But I also don't want to keep moving our little one around so much. Also Baby, I did read the requirements for out-of-state parole. I have to have a spouse, a grandparent, a parent, or an aunt/uncle who has resided in that state longer than 6 months. This is the requirement if I was to make the request straight after my sentence. However, I believe the process of me being home first and then making the request is a bit different, because ultimately, North Carolina has to accept me. As I said previously, Babe, I want to be home with you and home to me means wherever you are. But it would be smart for me to get established a little bit before I come down because I really don't want to feel like a burden to you. Make no mistake, Babe, if we went with option B, I'm gonna have my ass on that Greyhound or that Amtrak to come see my Baby. They don't be wanting niggas to leave the state without permission, but fuck that. We have a little more time to get things in order, but make sure you tell me what you would prefer and what you feel is better for our family, Sweetheart. Anyway Princess, I miss you a lot, Baby, I stay staring at your pictures on and off all day. Shit you was watching the news with me this morning before I went to work lol. To answer some of your other questions though, my family is doing okay, my sister still ain't got no job lmao. You know my mom's is still hanging in there, as always. As for myself, I have been doing good, Baby, which I owe to the constant encouragement and support I get from my wife. Shanna, you just don't know how glad I am about it almost being time to get the fuck outta here. Don't forget that I will be adding your moms house line to my phone list so I can hear your sweet voice when I want. I'll let you know when everything is approved so you can give me the days and times, Babe. Okay I want to ask you something and I want your honest answer. How does your mom feel about me and our relationship? I only ask because it seems as if she either don't like me or she is indifferent. Plus you never answered me before when I asked how her relationship was with dumbass. Because if she knew how he treated you. I hope she would be supportive of me knocking his shit off. Okay, Babe, enough of that and let me stop talking about your paper cause you really might send me some shit on a paper bag lol. I ain't forget neither, Love, so do expect a money order to come in the next couple of weeks, I told you I got you, Baby, it is my job to provide for you however I can, Babe, so don't argue with me. Damn our birthdays are coming up (smile). You grow wiser and more beautiful each year. Shanna, it has been a privilege to watch you grow into the amazing woman that you are. Well, Sexy, I will pause this moment for now, but loving you endlessly, Babe. Be careful and try not to let anyone or anything get to you, Sweetheart. Before I go, my Love, if there is anything that you need or if there is any way that I can keep that smile on your face, please don't hesitate to tell me, Baby. LaShanna, I love you so much and I want you to have a goodnight sleep. I am always thinking about you, Baby, you are the only woman that I will ever need. Kiss my Taylen and tell him I love him, Baby.

Loving you years ago and years ahead, Mr. Herring

7-27-2014

Song: Boyz II Men When I'm With You

Babe,

I got your letter on Saturday and I did write you back, but I started having thoughts that maybe you are getting overwhelmed by me writing so often so I threw it away. I don't know, Sweetheart, maybe I am my worst critic and my own enemy at times. But I do have concerns about things becoming routine and you gradually losing interest because of it. Anyway, Beautiful, it was good to hear from you (I can breathe now) lol. About our wedding, it sounds like you have everything laid out, shoot all I have to do is be there. Nah seriously, Babe I do like your ideas and after giving it some thought, I agree that we shouldn't go to court because I want our first and last wedding to be special for my Queen. We will need time to save, but I don't want to specifically say we need a whole year, Babe. It depends though, I mean do you want to be engaged for a year so we can save or is it because you want to see if our chemistry will last. I see you ain't waste no time mentioning your ring lol Baby, you know I got you (size 7) right? While I am on the topic, Sexy, I need you to tell me your bra, panties, sneakers, jeans, and shirt sizes (whew that's a lot) And don't be asking questions, Nosey. I just noticed that you still writing on this paper, come on, Babe, go to the store or I'll mail you some. Even without lines though, you still write nice and neat. Back to the wedding, I can't even name 20 people I like so our event will definitely be small and intimate. I think we should have it here because all my family is in NY/NJ, but I am willing to compromise. I am not sure either about your brothers walking you down the aisle. I would prefer your mom's if anyone. The venue and decorations are important, Baby, but what about our cake and honeymoon expenses? Oh and about the food seriously, Babe, do we have to feed them? Okay let me clean this parole thing up. If they do allow me to go to the half-way next year, Baby, I still won't be able to live at home until my max date, which is still 9-7-16. Brb…Brb, okay I'm back now Princess, I had to make my coffee. LaShanna, I am going to do everything possible to give you the wedding of your dreams, Sweetheart. So I am confident everything will go as planned. Allow me to also take this moment to make sure you know that under no circumstances, will I ever leave you, stop loving you, or working to keep our marriage healthy. I truly am in love with you, Baby, and I am yours. I intend to die that way. I can't believe it costs that much for Taylen's school. I mean I can see $165 bi-weekly, but every week. Babe, that can be rent for an apartment or mortgage for a home. I feel so guilty that you sold the couch, Babe. You could have at least got $550 (smile). Don't worry about it though because we will have all new things. Hell no don't sell the T.V, Baby, please, we can keep that one in our room and get a "70 inch for the living room (my man cave). You also should not be feeling like you are taking from me, Baby Girl. You complete me, don't you understand? You and Taylen are my family and my life. Knowing that you are without what you need, hurts me more than me going without. How can I look at myself in the mirror and call myself a man if my wife and child have to be deprived while I live comfortable? That shit is out. I want you to take pride in knowing that your man loves you enough to give you his very last, no matter the circumstance. Shanna, when I say that I will always be by your side and I will always support you in any and every way. So again, Boo, don't worry about it. I'll send more soon, Baby. I really appreciate you staying up so late to finish my letter, my

Love, cause I know you be having to get up and get our son ready for his day on top of all the other things that keep you busy. So thank you, Babe. On another note…. we say that a lot lol. About your funny stories, your gay friend is kind of dumb. Why the fuck would he call you about seeing a dead body (scary ass nigga). He should have called the boys. Babe, it kind of bothered me that some nigga was watching your comings and goings at the storage place, especially you being with Tay. He was clearly a dumb ass to believe you had a twin lol, I can't believe you really said that shit. And I can't even front that I was 'cheesin hard as hell' when you told him you was married and he saw my picture. Shanna, it feels good to be yours, Baby, I love you. Damn, I can't believe my birthday is really tomorrow! Where does the time go. It is always a bittersweet time of the year for me, but one thing I am grateful for is to have been able to have you almost every step of the way. Aside from all of this, how have you been feeling lately, Babe, mentally and emotionally? Have you decide when you want to start working again. I know how you feel about security already, so I do not expect you will seek employment there. I really want so much for you and Taylen. I just hope I am blessed with opportunity when I get home so I can give you that. I would rather die than to live on my knees and starve. I really could use a kiss and hug from my Baby Girl right now cause I'm missing you. Well, Beautiful, I will pause this moment in love with you for now, but I'll write again soon. Baby, I want you to be careful and know that I love you past the limits God can allow. Yes, I love you some more and some more and some more. I hope you find shelter in my heart and comfort in my thoughts, where I always keep you. Kiss my Taylen for me, I love you, Mrs. Herring.

Eternally Yours, Lance

Loving, Amazing, Sexy, Honest, Addictive, Witty, Nurturing. Smile for me baby

7-29-2014

Song: Miguel Simple Things

Sweetheart,

I swear that I am so blessed to have you in my life Babe. I don't even know where to begin because I am so caught off guard. I love my birthday card, Baby, I mean, damn girl, you really show how much you care about me. I really love this card, Shanna, the different shades of red and our royal color, gold that is fit just for me and you. Thank you so much, Babe, for taking the time to choose the perfect card and for the very sweet messages that you left on the inside for me. You should see the way I am smiling Boo, only you could have this effect on me. Omg this is so crazy, Everything in here fits our love story and no, Baby, there won't be a need for me to wonder how deep your feelings are for me. You always show me in the subtlest ways, but your actions speak volumes. Pumpkin, and I love you so much Baby. Shanna I have no idea where I would be without you, but I'm certain it wouldn't be where I need to be, which is with the love of my whole life. This feels amazing. This feels right. You know you got me wrapped around all of your fingers and pretty littles toes. I want to kiss you so bad. I love you,

LaShanna. Don't you let it cross your mind that there is anyone out there better for me than you, or that there will ever be a possibility of my affection and desire kept reserved for anyone else, but my wife. No way! no fucking how! Aight, Little Mama, onto your letter. I know from how everything sounds it may seem like a difficult process with my transition home, but we will work it out. Until I get a job, parole is going to be up my ass. But once I do, they won't require me to come in so frequently. However, in between that time, I will be coming down to visit you as well, Baby. I know you've been there almost two years, but you have to be my mom's or sister...etc. I will definitely try to pull their chain and convince them we are married to see if it works. But if I can't provide paperwork, it may be an issue. Honestly, Sweetheart, this is the only reason I mentioned us going to the courthouse. As previously stated, my Love, we are going to have our real wedding because it is a special day. The day I marry an angel from heaven and confess my love and devotion to her before God, a courthouse would cheapen everything. So you and your buddy was at the jewelry store huh. Baby, I will be more than grateful with whatever your choice is for my ring. But I like diamonds too, remember that. This is such a dream come true. Baby, that after all these years, everything we planned as kids, we are actually making it happen. Just to let you know, Babe, I only intended to be up here long enough for them to grant my

192

transfer to N.C. In case I can't get paroled right away, which only takes 6mos to a year. It isn't what I feel is the better plan, Baby Girl, its whatever "we" feel is better. But it will get worked out because I don't want to be away from my wife or our little one longer than I must. And hell yeah, I'm gonna let them niggas know I have a son in N.C.. About my mother- in-law, I am relieved to hear that she appears to be okay with me. I know besides my Taylen, she is the closest thing to you so I wanted her approval you know what I mean, Babe. I just want her to know how much her daughter means to me and that she is going to be taken very good care of. I got that Courtney Love for you, that crazy shit. But it's not like her disapproval or anyone else's would keep me from spending my life with you, Sweetheart. Anyway, Mrs. Herring, the card you got me and the letter it came with was unexpected surprise and they came right on time. You was counting the days too, huh Babe? Out of all of the birthdays I have had to spend away from home, this one was the best one I have had and I am glad I was able to spend it with you, Shanna, writing you, loving you, and thinking about you. So Beautiful, this will be all for now, but you really made my day. The only thing that can make it better is to look into your eyes and plant soft kisses on your body while your vagina massages my dick... mmm let me stop. I love you, Babe, and thank you again for making today special. Have a goodnight my Love, I will speak to you soon Sexy. Love Always Your Husband, Mr. Herring


7-29-2014

Song: Luke James Make Love to Me

Sweet Love,

I am so fortunate to have been able to call you today and hear your voice, Baby. You got me on a high that is so indescribable, Sweetheart, and it's funny how my Baby is the only person I got mail from on my special day. I miss how we use to stay on the phone all day, then once the batteries are low, we switch phones lol. Baby, even back then, I couldn't get enough of you and somehow after all of these years, that remains the same. I am sure you noticed a difference in how my sister calls you now (wink). I told you I would take care of it, Love. Shanna, I love the sound of your voice, so soft and full of life, music to my soul. It was turning me on listening to you snapping about what you not gone put up with and how you was setting people at the job straight lol, I'm like "yeah that's my baby" and she ain't having it. I ain't know that Taylen be at school that long, but them muthafuckas better be making sure nothing happens to him. Maybe I'll catch him next time cause I do miss him as well, just hearing him in the background is enough for me. For now anyway. Wait a minute, Boo, before I get too ahead of myself, I have something I want you to hear, okay? LaShanna, I am so proud of you, even when shit looks bad, you still try and make a difference, which is how I know everything is going to work out. Baby Girl, your husband admires your strength and the way you still hold shit down in the process of getting to where you want to be. I support you, Babe, a million percent. Your man is behind you and I believe in you. I know things are dragging right now, but our blessing is on its way. Sweetheart, God has a plan for us, you, and me. In the meantime, just do what you can to follow up on the status of the applications you have submitted because something will fall through. On my part though, I'm still gone provide financially for you the best way I can and as often as I can (don't even trip). I got you, Little Mama. But as I was saying before our call ended, you was not suppose to open Taylen's letter, punk. I can't believe he sat still long enough to let you read it. Deep inside, I am glad you did it, Babe, even if he doesn't quite understand everything yet. At least he'll know somehow his real father is here until I can be with you two physically. Since the letter ain't come yet about dumbass making you upset, let me just say if he not calling you about money, he don't need to call period. I don't even trust Taylen to be around him. I held my tongue out of respect for you but, Baby, I was livid when I found out he hurt himself in the bath when you were up here last. It is starting to piss me off just thinking about it, but I blame myself for not being home giving him his bath. Today was a good ass day, the best I could have considering where I am and I owe it to you, Shanna, so thank you Baby. I focused on nothing but being home with you, and being grateful because I am alive and spending my life with my Dream Girl. Not to mention reading my card a thousand times. I'm still gone read it some more, Baby. I love you with all my heart and thank you so much. I know you aren't too happy that your once a month came today, but I look at it as the rebirth of the strong woman you are. But I'll be there one day soon to make you hot tea and draw you a relaxing bath. It would have been nice to be there rubbing your back to make you feel better. You are going to be such a brat once I come home lol. Anyway, Princess, I'm pausing this unforgettable moment in time and still falling helplessly in love with you. I love you so much, Babe. You always know all the right things to do at all the right times. Have a goodnight sleep, Baby Girl, and know I am thinking about you. Love is love, Sweetheart, and yours is all I want. Be careful beautiful.

Loving you incessantly, Your Husband, Mr. Herring

You'll forever be a special part of me…mind, body, and soul.

7-31-2014

Song: Alicia Keys Girlfriend

LaShanna,

So nice to be writing you again, Sweetheart. You aren't going to believe this, but tell me why I was sleep, right? and in my dream, you were standing a few steps away from me smiling. But you was hiding something behind you. Then I woke up cause the police was tapping on the door to give me my mail (a letter from my Princess) you, of course. Now it has been cloudy as hell all day so I go to the end of the bed by the window so I can read better, and soon as I opened the envelope, the fucking sun comes out, shining bright as hell. That is the kind of stuff that makes me smile, reminding me that what you and I share is special. We are a match made in Heaven, Babe. It is good to know your grandma is healing properly and moving around and getting her exercise. It is such a relief, Boo. She is a very important part of our family tree. I could've sworn you had your 5k run the other week, but I'll make sure I do not forget the date again. Damn so I gotta wait that long for more pictures of my beautiful wife. I'm not tripping, Baby, I would wait an eternity for you. Yes, of course, I remember your numbers, there isn't much about you that is possible to forget. Maybe it is a good thing you don't always wear scarves to bed, they would only get in the way anyway (wink). Now as far as your little argument with son's father. That nigga is a bitch straight up. He talking about all he has is rent until employment comes. Well what the fuck, he could've sent half of that and then paid what he still owed on rent once unemployment came. I ask myself sometime what you could have possibly seen in a nigga like that, but I don't want you dwelling on shoulda, coulda, woulda's. I tell you what, if you really wanna fuck his head up, tell him Taylen may not be his. That will crush his ass, I promise you. For real, Baby, I just would rather that so you wouldn't have to deal with that bullshit. But isn't much you would give me the okay to rid us of this problem. Aside from that, I know you still sexy out there, but 17 nah son lol. You smell so good on this letter, Sweetheart, it makes me want you more ways than I can probably handle. Shanna, it's going to be hard for me to watch you get dressed in the mirror on the nights you have ladies night. Better believe, I'll be wide awake waiting for your fine ass to get home. I want you to make sure you keep me aware of any and everything that may bother you from time to time. Now that I look back on the way I vented some of my

frustrations about your ex, I realize I was being insensitive and I do apologize, Baby, I do. It is just extremely difficult for me to know someone is going out of their way to bring harm and discomfort to a woman I love so much, while my reactions are limited out of respect for that love. I am here for you though, Princess and will deal with whatever comes next. What I need though from you is your support for how I may decide to handle certain situations if I feel they are becoming too much for you. I need you to do a favor for me though, now I am not ignorant to the reality of things, but hearing you refer to my Taylen as his son, bothers me because he doesn't deserve Tay. Tay doesn't deserve the insult of being claimed by someone who does not care for him. Okay I need to switch gears cause I am getting pissed off about this. Anyway, my Love, I think I should end this one here for now because I am in a negative mental space. I love you, LaShanna, and I want you to enjoy the rest of your day, Babe. Drive safely and let our little one know I love him and miss you both.
Love Always Mr. Herring

To save you some aggravation, keep your communication with that nigga strictly on text message and if the messages aren't about him sending money, you don't need to respond period. Oh I'm not that tall baby, only 6'1. You are just a midget that's all, but you are my midget and I love you.

7-31-2014

Song:  Gerald Levert One Million Times
        Elle Varner Refill

Wifey,

Hey Pretty Lady, how are you feeling this morning Baby? As for me, I am still coming down off that high I have been on since speaking to you on Tuesday. I woke up with a smile on my face because a picture of you is the first thing I see. Then reality sets in that I am living out a dream because we are together, so I give you a kiss like I do every day. Baby, I wish I could sing lol cause I would sing to you. Yeah Boo, you got me open like that. I feel you smiling. By the time you get this letter, I hope the money made it to you. And after I situate the phone and set some aside for our calls, I will send you more. I know you may feel a little awkward, Babe, but I also know it may take some time for you to adjust to a man providing for you the way he should. Shanna, this don't mean you are giving me power over you or you are helpless. It simple means that you are accepting the due treatment, my Queen deserves (I love you). Anyway, my Love, I hope you haven't been driving yourself crazy with being bored and sitting in the house, maybe you should start on our wedding invitations. Your mother-in-law told me to tell you that you should see if there is a Xerox company down there because you can make a lot of bread with your degree in graphic design. She also said not to wait until the Post Office or Fire Department call you. Check their website from time to time for positions availabilities and you can call them with your test results as your advantage. One more thing, she said if you move back up here, she will give you an apartment if you get Section 8 (I'll explain later lol). Other than that babe everything has been going aiight, I'm just waiting on my next letter from you cause I'm feenin to read your words. I want to know, how Taylen doing in school? What exactly are they teaching him and is he still spitting on people? Speaking of my little man, you are probably going to pick him up in a couple of hours because I know he gets out at 4:30. Baby Girl, you need a serious break from the day to day stresses of maintaining a household and being a mother. I can't tell you enough how good of a job you are doing with my son. I believe sons get their strength from mothers and directions on how to use it from their fathers. So I commend you, Baby, again and again for all that you do. You want to know something Boo? Every time I have ever been asked to describe the perfect woman or what my type of women was, I always described you. I am so lucky and I know it. I mean damn, Baby, you are the kind of lady other women aspire to be, and it doesn't hurt that you look so fucking good. You must think I'm playing, but if you only knew how much I stare at your pictures all day. Tracing your lips with my fingertips, falling in love with that look in your beautiful eyes, and undressing you with mine. Before I forget to ask, how has your back been feeling lately? And what kind of car do you have? That was random right lol. I miss hearing your voice Sweetheart. I wish these couple weeks go by quick so I can start calling my wife. Look, Babe, I have a program to go to in like ten minutes so I need to start getting ready. I want you to know I love you and Taylen with all of my heart. Being able to call you, Mrs. Herring, is really a dream come true. I will talk to you later, Beautiful. Please be careful and make sure you give my son a kiss for me, Baby. Just when you start to feel like you are overwhelmed, remember that I am with you, my Love. You are not alone and never again will be. I love you, Babe. Love Lance, your Husband

7-28-2014

Child Support lol

Mrs. Herring,

Hey, Gorgeous, this won't be long because I just wanted something to send the money order with…I know it is not much, but hopefully, it will do until I can send you more…. kiss my son for me. I love you, Sweetheart.

Love Lance

8-8-2014

Part 1

Baby Girl,

I'm just getting both of your letters, Sweetheart and by the tone of this response, I'm sure you will know which one I read first. I do not even know where to begin because I am so hurt for you. I mean at first some of that ignorant shit Meerah was saying had me laughing at first, but it started pissing me off once that miserable bitch questioned what I can or can't be in my son's life. Then questioning my manhood, fuck that. So, I am going to address all that was said and hopefully give you some things to think about. Baby, everything, I have said or expressed my whole life since I knew you, before coming to jail. No, you don't know that I won't be fucking around while you are in NC until I get down there. You need to trust me the way I trust you are not fucking around while I'm locked up. You need to trust that I meant every word when I said you are the only woman I want, LaShanna. Baby, I would never risk losing a lifetime with you for 20 minutes with a random bitch. Sorry to disappoint your dumbass sister, but sex will absolutely not be the first thing on my mind. Getting my license renewed and working so I can visit and provide for you and Taylen are my priorities. I never been the type of man to chase pussy ever. It was here before me and will be here long after I am gone. I'm definitely not one of them weak-minded homo ass niggas, and you nor anyone else should ever be concerned about me fucking a man or vice versa. I was a devout Muslim at one time. Tell that bitch do not disrespect me. About me just saying anything so I can use you? lol, Honestly Sweetheart, what have I ever asked you for financially or otherwise? Let's not forget, I'm about to come home, it ain't like I got life. Tell that bitch a jailbird is one who repeatedly goes to jail. I only been here once. Tell that bitch I went to college, always held a full-time occupation and was almost a Sheriff and a C.O before this happened to me. I wasn't one of those filthy hood niggas she is used to dealing with. Don't marry me because I'm not gone have shit huh. She graduated from college and works a bullshit job and still lives in JC (what she got?) exactly? I really ain't even upset about what was said, Boo, it's more of the intent and mentality behind it. It's a shame that since a person never had a love like this, never really had any sincere man adore her, would be so negative about a person that is living their dreams. I mean if she said, "Shanna, just be careful cause he been gone for a minute", I would consider her looking out for your best interest. But because everything was so degrading and disrespectful, that's the shit I don't like, Babe. I will never care what other people see me as, so long as you see a good husband and my Taylen sees a faithful father, I'm straight Boo. This also isn't worth dwelling on so I'm gone start on Part 2 of this letter so I can open your other letter and write back to that too. I apologize for calling her a bitch, but I hope you understand. And you do know who visits me or if anyone writes that shouldn't because I tell you. Remember I told you how old girl popped up here and I told you every time I got a letter from her. I won't allow our love to be tainted by deceit, I have always been honest with you. I love you, Baby.

Love, Lance

8-8-2014

Song: Sam Smith Life Support

My Love,

I have had a chance to calm down some so I wanted to write you a Part 2 of that letter so I could focus on my wife without all the negativity. First and foremost, Baby, Congratulations on your interview with the Post Office. I have been praying about it since you said you took the exam. So, I am excited that you had a good interview. I also will pass the message to my mom's when I call home because I will be calling you tonight, Sweetheart. About the apartment, she just was saying that if you could get Section 8 to pay for it, she would give you an apartment if you needed it because relocating and finding a job may take a minute and she wouldn't want you worrying about rent. I wouldn't allow you and our son to be in Newark even though the block is safe. I would prefer the house in Hillside where I grew up. Let me also make clear that I have always loved you, Baby. I love you now and I'll love you 50 years from now. What I feel for my Baby Girl hasn't changed in 14 years and damn sure won't change when I'm home in 2 more. So, do I still want a wedding with you, the woman I have been in love with for so long? Hell fucking yeah! Shanna not even death can keep me away Baby, my heart and my love is all yours. Sweetheart, I promise you my life to learn and love you. There is nobody else for me, but you. God made you for me and I will not let you go because others don't believe dreams come true. What we share isn't too good to be true, Shanna, I have not invested all our time together to ruin it or to break your heart. I would never do you like that, Baby. But you will see in due time. I am proud to hear about all the progress Taylen is making in school, I'll be sending some books for him soon. Anyway, Princess, I am missing you a lot, I ain't get mail from you all week until today and began to worry so it's definitely nice to hear from you. I wanted to call you on your birthday, yesterday. But no one answered the phone at my house. By the way, we put the phone lists in next Thursday, so I'll be calling you directly. I don't want you to allow that conservation with your sister to stress you because everything is going to work out with us, Baby. I promise you Little Mama, I will not leave you and I would never cheat on you, Babe. I wish I could allow you to look through my eyes so you would at least have a glimpse at how obsessed and incessantly in love with you that I am. I seriously use to question my sanity, Baby, I literally think about you and being home with you every single day (all day long). I don't care what happens, my Love, I'm going to be at your side when all is said and done, Babe. You are my world, Shanna, my every hope, and the sum of my dreams is all in you. I'm staying with you and remaining faithful to you. I will be faithful mentally, emotionally, and definitely sexually. There is nothing that is worth me losing you and my Taylen. But I can show you better than tell you and I intend to do exactly that. It is about 6:45pm right now and I just went out to see if I could get you on 3 way, but nobody answering the phone and its pissing me off because it's an emergency, I have to call you and hear your voice. Bad enough the letter took 3 days to come, I need to know that you are okay because I am worried. Oh yeah, Beautiful, you never have to thank me for anything that I do for you and Taylen, but you are wrong. These are things I have to do because a man is supposed to provide for his family. Anyway, Sexy, let me take a look at a few things next week so I can see if there is extra so I can send you more. I put $50 on the phone already so I can call you once the numbers are approved. But when I get my receipt next week, I'll know my balance. Other than that, Princess, everything else is okay I guess; I find out my brother that's in the NFL got hurt so he won't be playing this year. That situation been bothering me on the low cause he never even reached out to tell us he made it, so I don't want him thinking now he in the NFL, everybody wanna keep in touch. So, it's complicated. Well my Love, I will be pausing here for now and still in love with you the way I always have been. I will get in touch with you before this weekend is out. Just how I'm trying, Baby Girl. I want you to please be careful and have a goodnight sleep, Babe, I love you so much, Mrs. Herring.

Love Always, Your Husband

Kiss Tay for me babe I love you.

8-9-2014

Song: Brian McKnight Back at One

Mrs. Herring,

Hey Beautiful, I hope you are feeling better emotionally since reading my other letter and I pray that you know in your heart that you are a permanent part of my life, Babe. Meaning, your position, will always be unchallenged. It is impossible to replace someone so perfect. You won't believe this shit; I went out again to call you and I got through, but some girl name Holly kept answering. So,

I'm on the phone arguing with this bitch that my wife's name is LaShanna, so please put you on the phone. Baby I could remember you wrote the right number when you sent mom's number. So, I came back and reread through some old letters and I see that the number is actually different than what I dialed. Okay now that I got all that out of the way, Baby, it was a very pleasant surprise to open your second letter and sex pictures inside, as well as entries from your old diary. Shanna, you are so damn gorgeous, and I love the sweet messages you be leaving on the back of the pictures and envelopes. Your hair grew fast as hell, Babe, and you were looking so classy and sexy for your interview and yes (licking my lips) that ass is priceless. You want to know something, Sweetheart, my favorite pictures are the ones where you show me your stomach, I am literally going to kiss your everywhere from head to toe and in between, especially your stomach, Babe. Your body is not only beautiful to me, it is perfect. So I don't like that you said, "at least my face is still pretty though" because everything about you that I'm looking at is pretty. I do appreciate you sharing yourself with me like this, Baby. It means a lot to me, but damn you banging as hell. So that's the look you gonna give me when I say I'm going out huh lol. Boo, I'm scared just by looking that once you put that sugar on me, I won't ever wanna go nowhere. I should be standing behind you in these pictures, one hand on the front of your thigh and my other holding your waistline pulling you closer to me and wishing our bodies could melt together in those moments. I see Taylen face too. It's time for another haircut too. I really pray you haven't changed your mind about wanting to marry me, Love, after all that nonsense because the truth is and will always be that I cannot live without you, LaShanna and I love you, Mama for real. I think us marrying on 7-7-17 is better because the first two sevens symbolize my birth month, your birthday and if you add things up, the last two digits symbolize the 17 years we will have known one another and how long I have been in love with you. Damn, I thought I was being slick and forgot you saying you wanted no T.V in our bedroom. Come on, Babe, please. I'll watch 'First 48' with you and 'Dateline'. As far as the parole, what I really want to do is come home and renew my license, get a job so I can save a few thousand, then transfer to NC with you and my Taylen shortly thereafter. I would like to get paroled straight from here to there, but because we are not married, they will not allow it. At least the other way with me working and staying focused, my parole officer will see I'm handling my business and be more willing to help me transfer, which only takes 6 months to a year from the day I request it. I also want to be on my feet a little bit financially because I don't want to put any burdens on you, Baby, especially not after everything your sister said about me using you. Baby Girl, I never want to take anything from you. I only want to add to your life and happiness because if I can't do that, I have no purpose. I really believe we are meant to be and that I am supposed to do all I can to take care of you and Taylen and that is my dream and my greatest aspiration. I am going to do all I can to get us together as fast as I can, but I always want you to say how you feel about things, and if you know a better way, Baby, please share it with me.

Shanna, I am willing to do whatever I have to so that we can be together. I need my Princess. Please stop saying that too, Babe, because for me not to accept Taylen is for me not to accept you and that shit is out. I am always thinking about my wife, missing you, and wanting to be anywhere you are. This will all be a memory soon and you will be laying in my arms getting your face kissed gently. I want to give you massages and make love to you after long days at your job. Washing your legs and your back when you are in the bath, candles lit, music low, and sipping your champagne. On those days when you are frustrated or being snappy is when I will take you by your hand into our bedroom, pinning you against the walls to kiss you. Then laying you down locking you down so you can't squirm and fucking the shit outta you until the stress is gone. You can release your frustrations on my tongue and all over my dick. Baby, I've never wanted anyone the way I always want you, Sweetheart (never). Shanna, you can count on me, my Love not to let you down or break your heart. I know I have something special at home and, Baby. I promise, Boo, I don't want anyone but you. You'll see once I'm home. My mother raised a good man for you, Sweetheart, so please don't doubt me. If there is ever anything you can think of that I can do to show you I am all yours, Baby Girl, do not hesitate in telling me. I would do anything for you, LaShanna. I don't want anything out in them streets because nothing compares to what I have in you. So, Gorgeous, this is all for now, but I hope you get my letters soon and that your heart smile like mine does when I think of you. I love you so fucking much, Baby, you really got me whipped, beat, nose open and all the above, LaShanna. I won't let anything destroy what we are building because you are all that matters. Let's just let God continue to guide us the way he has been. I know we will wind up exactly where he wants us, Boo, together. So, this is how I'll end things for now, still loving you and never giving up under any circumstances. Be careful in your travels, Sweetheart, and enjoy your day Beautiful. I love you, Mrs. Herring, and will call home so I can speak to you as soon as I can arrange it.

Loving Only You, Your Husband, Mr. Herring

It makes me smile reading your old diary. Baby, this is meant to be. What we have is special and unbreakable. The devil is always busy trying to ruin God's blessings, but

I'm not having it. I can't lose you and my Taylen. I might as well lose my life.

8-10-2014

Song: Ciara Promise

Beautiful,

I pray these words reach you in good spirits and are greeted by your amazing smile. Baby, you mean way more to me than I can express and oftentimes words escape me in my attempts to explain how grateful I am to have your divine presence in my life. I was just sitting here last night flipping through the channels and paused for a minute to ask God to help me let go of the anger I had over the things your sister said. Then I asked for a sign so I would know things will work out between us. Since I began to feel you may have been having second thoughts of marrying me. This next part put me in shock and almost made me cry. Yes my tough ass lol. After praying I opened my eyes and didn't realize I stopped absentmindedly on TLC before I prayed. So, there was a girl on there trying on wedding dresses. Her last name was the same as yours, Babe. Crazy right? Anyway, my Love, I got another letter from you today with the words of inspiration you sent me. Thank you, Sweetheart. My mail was late by two days because I was moved to another unit so my door could be fixed, and although I came back these dumb asses ain't update the file on time so my mail got sent there. But I have everything now so don't worry, Boo. By the way, I did see a letter from my mother when I opened the mail yesterday. No, babe, I ain't read it. I immediately got an envelope, addressed it, and mailed it out. She came to see me earlier, so she knows it is on the way, she was smiling, Babe. I also spoke with her about what was said, and she was basically referencing one of my cousins who always be in everybody business and is miserable with her own so she can't sincerely be happy for anyone else. Anyway, though I have a lot on my mind because of all the bullshit going on out there with my brothers and sisters. But aside from that your, hubby is good. I am the happiest I have ever been, and I am just enjoying our time together. Making plans and building a solid foundation with the woman I love. I completed this program recently; they basically show you how to handle job interviews with having a criminal background and things like that. I mean its commonsense shit to me because I always kept a full-time job. Serious though, Baby Girl, I love you and I love being with you. I appreciate you taking the time to write me those encouraging words. You are right, my Love; our love story is true life and I like being able to live out every chapter with my Princess. Shanna, you brighten up my life so much and you don't even understand Babe. I'll never let you go. You are so nosey; I knew you would try and snoop and see why I asked for your clothes sizes. Chill, Boo, I got this. I have many things in store for you, Mrs. Herring. You know I would do anything to keep you happy, Sweetheart. I keep glancing over at a picture of you as I write, somehow not being able to keep my eyes off you. Shanna, you are beautiful Babe, all over. Everything about you is like a magnet to me, keeping my emotion and attention focused on you. I wanna kiss your hands softly, then nuzzle my nose across yours like the Eskimos do, before I look you directly in your pretty eyes and kiss your sweet smile. I will be so glad to be home with you listening to music and helping you cook in the kitchen. I can see me now watching you bend over to check on food in the oven, thinking "Damn, my wife ass is so fat". I can't wait to clean the house and put Taylen to sleep". Well my Queen, I hope you have been okay and getting enough rest. You know I always worry about my little Mama. But look, Sunshine, I will pause this one here for now missing you so much and falling more and more in love with everything about you. Tell Ms. Lynn I said hello and please tell our little one I love him. Baby, thank you for being you, a part of life I cannot be without. I love you so much, Baby and meant what I said. After the dust settles, I'll still be here remaining loyal and faithful to you. I love you so much, Babe, have a goodnight.

Love Lance

8-11-2014

Song: Sisqo Incomplete

Baby Girl,

I must have read the pages of your diary over one hundred times this weekend my Love. It always brings me back to a simpler part of my life, when things were good, and my only responsibility was to go to school and keep my room clean. Although we both know I had a hard time with that because my ass stayed on punishment. Boo, it is a refreshing and loving feeling I get because every time I look back over my life, you were always at the center of my special moments. I can remember being in my room talking to you and playing the game, and when there were times that you weren't home, or we couldn't speak. I would always call the loop and listen to my baby's messages over and over again (my account was #25713).

Shanna, I will take no amount of time with you for granted, Sweetheart. I have waited almost my entire life for what is now unfolding between us. With you, is where I have always wanted to be Baby. Without you, I would have no proof of special memories of a life lived before things got crazy. Without you, Babe, there would be no future for me or a promise that God would smile on me one day. I hope you won't get tired of hearing it because I won't stop letting you know that I love you, LaShanna. Having said all of this my love, you should know I am here for you and that my intentions with you and our family are sincere. How could I ever turn my back on you? Contrary to outside opinions, my wife is going to be treated the way a queen should and loved beyond my last breath. By the way, Babe, mom said Congratulations on your interview, I forgot to mention it, but I told her about it. My mother is kind of reserved unless I ask her a question flat out, but she likes you. You already know that, and she is incredibly supportive of our relationship Babe. Anyway, Beautiful, I wonder what you did today and where you are as you read my letter. How that song goes? ♫ *"I know you've seen a lot of things in your life", that got you feeling like this can't be right", but I won't hurt you, I'm down for you baby"* ♫. These are words my heart is singing as I stare at your pretty face in between writing my words. I wonder at times how my Taylen will act once I get home. Whether he'll be standoffish or accepting of me because I love that little boy so much and I'm willing to earn his trust. I see a lot of you when I look at him. His eyes light up when he is smiling, like yours do, Plus he's got that same big head. Back to you though, Sexy. What are you doing and how have you been feeling, Baby? Make sure you let me know the times when I can call you, because I don't want your mom's cursing me out for calling and make sure she knows I am paying for them. Since we are on the subject, how is your mom's doing? Like, does she seem happier down there than in Jersey? I don't really know the details of why she left water boy, but I'll buss his ass if she feels it needs to happen. I even remember she worked at Jordache (smile) I remember everything, Boo. Genuinely being in love with a woman like you made me want to learn every detail about you. See Princess, you had me from the very start, and you will have me until the end, babe. What have you been cooking lately too? cause you not gonna 'Digiorno me to death'. How is your progress at the gym? I know you not going crazy or doing shit that can hurt you. Oh, yea, I know niggas be eyeing you in there. You better tell them 'bullets and muscles don't mix'; You know I don't play about you. Shit I still wanna fight the nigga who grabbed your ass in the stairwell back in 9th grade for real babe. Aight, Pumpkin, I have to get ready for work so let me go for now. Shanna, I love you and I hope you and my son are doing okay. I am missing you both so much. If you are going out for anything, please be careful, Babe and have a good day, my Heart. I love you, Mrs. Herring.

Love Always, Lance

Wrote on 8-13-2014
Sent on 8-15-2014

LaShanna,

I was trying to be positive about the situation but the more I think about this bullshit, the more pissed off I am getting. So, since I have been feeling the same since reading that letter Saturday, I'm going to tell you how I feel, and you can either fix it or let the cards fall where they may. How dare you let those bitches (especially Meerah) pass judgement on me and suggest the dumb shit you allowed them to suggest? Then to actually listen to the shit long enough to allow it to affect you. Everybody is entitled to whatever their opinion is, but for you not to defend me, that is fucked up and I am disappointed by that. You were with a sorry ass nigga for over a year before he began to show you who he really was, and this was someone you spent actual time with. But me, who has been the same fucking person for years without us meeting, don't get the benefit of the doubt. So yea now I'm back on the defensive because clearly you won't defend me. It is a big ass difference in you debating reasons why our relationship will work, and you putting that bitch in check for saying that bullshit she said. Again exactly what you did not do. The one thing I don't get is for it to be said "he is probably using you and saying what you wanna hear because he is locked up", because what does that bitch think you are sacrificing for me. Once again, I don't press you for visits, never asked you for money, or any of that. I pay for when I call you, so really, what do you bring to the table that she thinks I am taking advantage of…Nothing. You had a whole baby with another man and you are the one living ten hours away. I am the one shifting my life to accommodate these things, not you. But even knowing that shit, you still let that whore kick my back in. No matter what I do, it doesn't seem to be good enough and I'm getting tired of that shit. Since she knows every fucking thing about me and my bad intentions, does she know Alvin was two steps from beating your fucking ass. Does that bitch know, he drives around in the car he drives, while you are fucking stuck paying for a baby you ain't make alone? I don't want to hear that bullshit about he not working cause his car insurance is paid somehow. But nah them hoes ain't investigating that instead they popping shit about me and your silly ass is really feeding into it. I know you was because you said, "What they said bothered me cause those were fears I had before", which was also news to me cause I never knew you feared I might be a homo. I would have never let anyone say none of that shit you say to me since there has never been any action on your part. I believe you believe I trust you, but clearly that respect is not extended to me. I am that same nigga and I don't mean that punk ass $100 dollar nigga using my resources to help lighten your burden. I'm that motherfucker who never had an adult life to experience life on my own but was willing to sacrifice it to accommodate your family. But you ain't tell that bitch any of that. "Don't marry him. He's not gonna have shit". Well if it's like that then, maybe they're right. But I damn sure don't remember calling either one of them hoes when your rent couldn't be paid, or when your car got totaled. I have raised this issue more than once as far as the sacrifices you do and don't make, so now until I feel things are equal, we can pause this whole situation. If I wanted to be with someone that I would have to defend myself against their family while my dumb ass keeps trying to show I am not a dog, I would've stayed with the last bitch. "He gone be fucking bitches when he come cause sex is the first thing on his mind," I thought I told you before if it was pussy I wanted, I could get it without wasting my time or anyone else building a life with someone for it. You should've stood up for me because it was your fucking job to do so. Do them bitches know you let Alvin spend the fucking night at your house and I ain't question you once about it. Of course, not. But I'm the one you need to be weary of huh? You always say I be going back in forth, but it's you. You are indecisive, contradictive, and obviously easily swayed by bitches who don't know me. So yea I'm mad as hell at your ass. I'm holding you responsible so you can either fix this or don't. It's not my job to tell you how. Just know I'm keeping you at arm's length until I see a change. I'm done with the talk. Let's see some action from you now. Since I am being 100 with you. Let's me know that I am aware of a few things. It is an exceedingly small world and I don't be tripping over shit because I'm grown, but don't insult my intelligence either.

L.

I had second thoughts about mailing this but since I'm still pissed the hell off 2 days after I wrote it, and for whatever reason, you ain't write me since sending me that letter, it is what it is. Those letters you got before this and probably responded to have nothing to do with you not saying shit since 8-4-14 when you wrote me that letter about your trifling miserable ass sister.

8-15-2014

Song: Montell Jordan Must Have Been
Luther Vandross All My Love

Mrs. Herring,

Hello beautiful it's about time I heard from you lol, I'm
laughing as I write because I know your face is tense as
hell after reading my first letter to you. I just hope you
read that one first instead of this or I miscalculated the
days. It should be obvious my Love you know I was only
playing Boo. I told you I would get that ass back. Shanna,
you know in real life that your husband would never speak
to you like that. Plus, if I even thought that Alvin faggot
ass jumped at you, I would plant him. Anyway,
Sweetheart, I have been calling my house all week so I
could try and get my baby on 3 way, but no one has been
home during the hours when I'm out. I did speak to
mom's earlier but that was brief because she was in the
middle of packing up for her trip to Vegas. She said to tell
you she got your letter, but she wouldn't tell me what you
wrote. My mother respects you as a young woman and
she thinks we are meant to be together. Okay Princess,

now to address some of what you said in this letter. I'm upset that homegirl at the post office did not make it known that she found someone else for the spot, but don't be discouraged, Baby, maybe God has something better for us. I am kind of surprised that your letter to me is so short especially because it's the only one I got since before your birthday. Babe, what is going on? Is something wrong that you aren't telling me? You know I can't help if I don't know. Now my Love about our wedding? I already told you, Sweetheart, I want to marry you now; shit I think the 14 years I've waited so far is too long. My only concern with a wedding was us being able to afford it. I really do not want to be away from you and I don't want to be away from my Taylen any longer than I have already had to. While I am up here, I want to get my license then after that it's a wrap. I figure I should be on my feet in 6 months to a year and after not being in trouble along with that, I'll be able to move easier. I don't want to wait until I move to NC before we get married though. Seriously, Baby, I think you are dancing around a little. Just tell me what you want to happen and when you want it to happen as far as our marriage and we will do that. Shanna, I can't stress it enough how bad I want you to be my wife on paper. Why postpone something I've always wanted to share with you, and I mean just you Babe. I hate knowing that you are going to sleep in a bed every night without me, in a home that is not ours, so just let me know, Pumpkin. I feel bad because of the tone of your letter. I know you feel alone Baby, but we only have 24 months left and it's over. Besides, there is a possibility of me going to the halfway house sometime next summer. Shanna I am coming home my Love and I'm coming home to you and our little one. Please don't feel down. Good news, Babe, I put the phone list in this morning so I will be calling you directly in the next week or so, once you tell me what days. Other than that, Beautiful, everything has been okay. I have just been worrying about my Queen so far away from me. I must say again how much I like these pictures. You don't have to worry about someone else getting them. By the way, I can get any pictures you send me as long as you don't put your fingers or anything else inside of my flower, I can have it lol. Okay, Sexy, it is getting late so I will pause here for now, loving you more than I did yesterday. Be careful, Baby, and try not to stress, okay. I will call you on Sunday or Wednesday, my Love, because I need to hear your voice, I am missing you so much. Oh, shit I forgot my mother said she'll be forwarding the house calls to her cell phone. Well I love you with all my soul, LaShanna, and I need you to stay strong Little Mama, we are almost there. I love you, Baby Girl.

Love Mr. Herring

Kiss my son and tell him I love him please. My house number, Babe, call my mother whenever you get time and check on her for me please, Baby. I don't know if you'll need this for our wedding stuff, but you are my wife and I think you should have this, my social security. You better not lose it punk. I love you, Shanna and I am there with you, Baby, every time you close your eyes.

8-18-2014

Song: DJ Khaled ft. Chris Brown I'll Hold Down

Sweetheart,

When my letter finally reaches your pretty eyes, I hope you are feeling better than you were in your last letter, Babe. I know you are still somewhat unfamiliar with your surroundings, regardless of being there for two years. You really don't have anyone who can relate to you on a personal level and on top of that a career opportunity hasn't presented itself yet, but it will. Things are going to turn around, Baby, and soon will get better than they seem at the moment. You have people who love you so much, Baby, especially me, so don't allow yourself to feel alone.

It can be draining and emotionally exhausting wanting me to be home now instead of waiting longer, but I'm coming Baby. I have already begun taking steps to show you that it all will have been worth the wait. I been on my stalker shit staring at a picture of my wife and was interrupted because I was called to the mail room. Sweetheart, when I got there, I was way more anxious just to see your name in the sender section, than I was to actually see what was in the bag. So, I want to thank you for thinking of me, Baby Girl, thinking of me enough to get me a book by my favorite author. You probably don't know it, my Love, but you are the only person that actually bought me something on my birthday in 10 years. I am smiling at how much I love you. I haven't heard from you much over the past week and I do miss you a lot, Shanna, I just want you to be okay and I want for my Taylen to be taken care of. I been listening to some Anita Baker mix that is playing, so you already know I can't take my mind off you, Princess. It's like these singers be stealing pages out of our love story to write they songs, but I'll be damned if it doesn't feel good inside knowing I can relate to these sweet words because I am living them with you. The phone list I put in should be approved at least by the end of next week. Shit, it ain't like I got mad numbers, just you, mom's, and grandma house. Remember after our house caught fire and we lived here, she used to be kicking a nigga off the phone. Babe, I'm happy you are the woman

I am in love with and spending my life with. I have wanted to be with you for so many years that at times this doesn't feel real. I want to go somewhere special on our first date and I want it to be romantic and something memorable. Anyway, Mrs. Herring, what have you been up to, Love? You better enjoy these last few weeks of summer cause it's almost over. One more Summer to go, Baby, one more Christmas and Thanksgiving after this, and it's finally over. You gonna be laying on me and we gone talk about this when we look back. I can almost see you giving me this serious look telling me "You better not do that shit to me again", I swear I can hear your voice deep in my mind's eye. Yep it's almost time for me to turn up on the workout, I said when I had exactly two left, I was gone start getting busy so. Oh, yea I forgot to tell you Baby, that last letter you wrote me smelled so fucking good. I had to go in, I couldn't help it, Boo. I'm glad I opened my eyes in that split second because I almost came on your letter. It never shot that far before. LaShanna, I more than love you, Pumpkin, and I am really one million percent invested in our marriage as well as your happiness. I can't get enough of you, Sweetheart, "You got that Southern stuff I like", Anthony Hamilton song. Even through written word, you make it so easy communicating with you. There is no other woman I would ever want this connection with. I love our relationship. Okay, Sexy, hopefully I will get a letter from you today, but if not, I will still write to you again later on my Love. So, I will pause briefly here for now. Adoring you so much, Babe. I love you, Shanna and you will hear from me again soon, Baby Girl. Make sure you hug Taylen for me and tell him that I love him. Be safe my love and know you are always being thought about by me. I love you, Mrs. Herring. Love Always, Your Husband,Mr. Lance Herring

8-19-2014

Song: Anita Baker More Than You Know

Beautiful,

Hey Baaaby, lol, just I predicted I got a letter from you, Sweetheart, and you smell sooo good, Babe! What are you trying to do to me? I got all of the pictures you sent me and put them in your photo album immediately. Thank you because you know I love looking at your sexy ass. Yes Boo, you was looking unbelievably beautiful on your birthday. I like that shirt you are wearing with them funny pockets lol. Them jeans! good lord, them jeans! I would have loved peeling them things off you that night. Shanna, you have such a beautiful smile. You was cheesing too which means you were probably laughing while you were taking the picture. Your cousins though? them niggas look country as hell. But they look like we would have a lot of fun together. It's crazy, but seeing the shorter one, makes me miss being big a little. Question is one of them the cousin that use to say since he was your uncle, he could beat you with a belt. Damn, I just realized I been calling them your cousins. It is such a relief to see your family, Babe, because I always be scared that if something happens God forbid you are all alone. But I know it's not the same as having me there. I like your shoes to, Mrs. Herring, those flats was looking fly on you! Check my Baby out. Speaking of babies, what happen to my son's eye? It looks like he got a small scar over his left eye lid. Why is he eating that funny ass grape lollipop? I hate grape. Sweetheart, you do not need to be giving him no haircuts either. Omg I have to hurry up and come home. About your Aunt, she looks cool as hell. Shit, Meerah don't like nobody so if you fucks with her, I fucks with her. Baby, are you going to her wedding ceremony? If so, let me know how it was. Damn, Sweetheart, you got a nigga real thirsty. I can't wait to wrap my arms around you. I love you so much and I'm keeping you forever and seven days. I just realized I ain't respond to nothing in your letter yet, Honey, give me a minute. That was quick, I wish I would've known the phone was back on instead of arguing with Holly, because you got one digit wrong lol. I know you want to move out and it will happen, Sweetheart, just budget the money carefully and be patient. What you mean you driving yourself crazy about our wedding. I told you, we ain't have to wait, but you might be talking about the ceremony my bad. No, I'm not throwing your diary pages away. They are a testament of our love together, and if you try to throw them away, we gone box. Babe, you can take a nice deep breath because I am here to stay and I will be a permanent father to Taylen, I love him and I love his mom so much, she is my world. You are wrong about one thing, Princess, we want to be together so bad and with God and family, we are gonna see it. In my eyes, our life as one, has already begun and once we come together physically, it will feel right to you. We are going to make it, Shanna, because you have a dedicated man who is interested in nothing else but being with you and staying that way. I am absolutely looking forward to these candlelit dinners and cuddling together, especially the bubble baths. I hope we get a big bathtub because we are going to need it. Damn, Little Mama, you smell so good, I'm trying to behave today but I really like this prayer that you sent love, and I am going to learn it so I can include it in my prayers about us. You are a real woman Shanna, and I never had that before. I had little girls pretending to be women or women that behaved like little girls. So, it means so much to have met you and been given the privilege to love you so I would know the difference. There is no way in hell I would even disrespect you or cheaper our bond by doing anything with another female. Baby, all I want is you. Okay Love, there is something I want to tell you and I hope it doesn't make you upset. When I got your letter today it also came with a letter from my ex. I don't know why the fuck she wrote especially since I made it clear to her I wanted to be left alone back when she popped up on the visit back in January. I did not open the letter, Baby, I seen the name and ripped it in four pieces then dropped it into the toilet. I just wanted you to know because we are together and we are getting married. And I never want to keep nothing from you. Anyway, Beautiful, this will be all for now because I want this all to go in the mail tonight so its gets to you quicker. Thank you so much for the pictures you sent me of my Queen. Baby, I love you and I want you to have a goodnight okay? I am such a lucky man to be spending my life with an angel. Mrs. Herring, I love you, Baby Girl and still missing you endlessly.

Love Lance

8-20-2014

Song: Nicki Minaj Your Love

Beautiful,

I just got a letter from you, Sweetheart, which is a little
ironic because I just put something in the mailbox for you
about our wedding stuff. Babe, you should've seen me just
now. I heard the nigga doing the mail and I closed my eyes
tight as hell like, "please let me hear from my Baby,"
"please let me hear from my Baby." I am a little surprised
at how late this one actually came now that I see the date
you wrote it. But I'm happy to hear from you, Sweetheart.
Sounds like you had a busy ass day doing all that running
around, and thank you again, Love, for the pictures you
sent me. Shit, I wish you would have said you was low on
stamps because I would have sent you some. Babe, it's
good to give charity. Only when we don't need it
ourselves. Don't forget this wedding won't pay for itself.
Now you talking about donuts, I never had a Krispy
Kreme anything, and you make the shit sound so good,
I'm scared to try it now. Sorry to disappoint, but no,
Princess, you can't send me a dozen here. However, I'll
be glad to eat as many as you feed me once I get home. I
want LaShanna flavor. I am not sure about the Witches of
Cast End; I think it comes on Lifetime, so I'll see what's

it about. I figure I'd get use to these shows now since you gonna punish me anyway when I'm home. You stay teasing me, laying in bed with just a t-shirt and panties huh. It is sweet agony, Baby, tease me some more and nah it will only seem like you are wearing too much once I'm laying next to you. You had me bugging the way you talked about them people driving down there. Shit, tell Pookie I need a license renewal. Not to change the subject, but I'm not tripping off Meerah. She has always been dismal and negative. What's going to be a trip is when she finally figures out a woman will do her dirtier than a man. It really don't surprise me that she is gay, since her experiences with men haven't seemed to be too meaningful. Okay, Baby, listen to me this next part isn't so easy for me to express without letting my anger or jealousy interfere so much. Now I appreciate that you was upfront with me about Raymond, but I was unaware that he told you he loved you or that what was said confused you enough to where you had to question if you was supposed to be with me or him. Because you told me he was only a friend, and you never said feelings was involved. So honestly, did you ever have feelings for him babe? Is that who you would want if I wasn't in the picture? My feelings are a little hurt that I am asking my wife, the only women I can truly, wholeheartedly loved, if she has intimate feelings for another man. I don't want to be handled or lied too. I hate knowing that there is a lingering possibility that I could ever lose you and Taylen, especially after all of this. I really have given you the rest of my life, Baby. Since we are on the subject, I think it's funny you say God was testing you because I kept asking myself yesterday, "Why the fuck that girl still wrote me after I made it clear I was finished with her and in a beautiful new relationship. I actually cursed her out , but it crossed my mind that maybe I was being tested because all the other times I fell for that shit. This time I passed because I read your letters to me over and over then flipped through your photo album. Only stopping to tell your pictures how much I love you and that I won't allow anyone or anything to come between us. Baby, I believe that prayer is strengthening our bond and our relationship. God is very involved in our union because we are made for one another, you for me and I for you. I told you a few letters ago that things would get better financially, but Bae if they sent you one big ass check, please put some aside for a rainy day. Please do not talk about God calling you to be with him cause my heart can't even take the thought of that shit. I will never be able to prepare for that one. I wish you would have told me I could read that letter before I mailed it to her. Soon as I saw the introduction I was like nope this is between my wife and her mother-in-law. Baby, I love you so much. You are just an amazing woman all around and I won't ever be leaving you, Princess, not in thought, word, or deed. I used to think people were stupid when I would hear it said, "be glad you woke up this morning," cause I could not see what the hell was so grand to be glad about. My perspective now has changed so much because I look at each day as another privilege to learn you and love you better. Shanna, I have you on such a high pedestal and no one else could ever or has even come close. I honestly feel deep in my heart that if loving you is the only true love I ever experience, your love is the only love I needed. I appreciate your liking the person I am and helping to mold the man I am constantly becoming. Even if according to my sister I act like P from Baby Boy lol. Well, Pumpkin, the sun is beginning to set, the sky is a pretty pink blend of pinks, purples, and oranges. That is where I want to make love to you, Babe, right in the midst of those clouds. So, let me go for now, Beautiful. But you already know I'll be writing you again soon, my Love. LaShanna, I love you from the bottom of the ocean to the top of the heavens, Babe, and can't wait to be next to you.

Please continue to smile on the outside so I can smile on the inside. I love you Mrs. Herring. Kiss my little man for me and be safe sweetheart.

Loving Only, You Mr. Herring

I have a distant memory of my Goddess. When she smile, it took my breath away. We are in a rapture of love, so to be honest, in any direction we go, my love is here to stay.

8-22-2014

Song: Trey Songz Fumble

Baby,

Well I'm just getting this letter from you and I'm not sure whether to be satisfied about getting you back or to be worried because you are taking what I said serious. Let me try to explain, but I swear I'm gone be so mad if this is another one of your jokes. I expressed to you the first time how I felt about what Meerah said. When have you ever known me to bite my tongue or save something for later that I'm pissed about now? I just figured since it was a recent issue, it would be more effective, rather than me making it like yours was, which you would have seen coming. Come one now, Sweetheart. I did send both of those letters the same morning so if I was trying to just make it seem like I was playing, why wouldn't I have just avoided it altogether by not sending it period? I don't like that you did not include our last name on your envelope, and I'm scared of what the lyrics to this Marsh Ambrosius song could be since your letter isn't a happy one. You are funny as hell. I felt good after getting that off my chest. Okay I may have gone a little too far in some of what I said, but do you honestly feel like I was trying to hurt you. On top of that, Babe, I specified that I was not referring to that punk ass $100 dollars, and you honestly think I want it back? Can we please not do this. I feel even worse because you do so much for me, Shanna, too much for me to make you feel I was throwing it in your face. I apologize because that was definitely not my intention. Then you got my babies, yes plural you and Taylen sitting in that hot ass car and it's my fault. Baby, please forgive me cause I ain't anticipate things going this far. I'm sorry, Pumpkin, seriously please don't be upset with me. I did not mean to make it seem like I was throwing the little that I try to do for our family in your face. What kind of man would I be to do that? Now I feel stupid because I just sent you an idea for our ceremony, but I'm scared you may be having second thoughts now because of this. Anyway, my Love, I sent my social security because I may need a checking account not to mention, we will eventually need life insurance, plus Babe, I just felt as my wife, it was something you should have. You're not that kind of girl, seriously Babe. Why would something like that even cross my mind. Listen Love, I am going to cut this one short because it doesn't feel good writing under these circumstances. I do love you though, Shanna, and you already should know how much I love my Taylen. I told you regardless of what happened, nothing can make me leave you two or change how I feel. Again, I really am sorry for making you feel anything less. Have a good night, my Love, and I pray you will feel different when I hear from you again. Be careful, Sweetheart and kiss our little one for me since I'm not there yet to do it myself. I love you.

Love Always Then and Now Lance

Today is bad all around. It's the day, 8 years ago when I caught this case, and even though you are upset with me, Baby, your letter is the only thing I smiled about today. I love you.

8-23-2014

Song: Ginuwine My Whole Life Has Changed
        Etta James At Last


Mrs. Herring,

Baby, the way I felt when I walked in and saw you for the first time is priceless. I always felt that you were the most beautiful woman my eyes ever saw. But Baby, seeing you up close and personal is so much more. I miss you so much already, I never thought I could obsess over you anymore than I have all of these years, but I am so wrong. I will never forget the sweet taste of your lips or that amazing feeling I got from touching your soft skin, Babe. Your body fits so perfectly in my arms, Baby, it was really a dream come true to finally know the comfort of your embrace. I was so happy to see you, Princess and I thank you so much for the surprise. I kept putting my head down to wipe my eye to keep tears in that were trying to fall. I couldn't let you see me cry, Babe. Then looking back and forth between your pretty ass smile and those thick thighs was making my dick hard. Which is why I extended my legs those few times. Shanna, I love how you never really let my hands go, even if you were making a gesture with your hand, you would hold both of my hands in your other one. I love you so much for that. The next time I will make sure I have a haircut and shape up, because I was looking busted. I was so nervous, Sweetheart; I was like damn I hope she still thinks I look good and ain't just trying to be nice about it. Then you gone ask if we seriously gonna get married, Boo, you know I'm yours forever. It was our first time so we was both a little nervous, but that kiss was all fireworks to me. It killed me to let you go, Baby Girl, but I kept my eyes focused on you until I lost you in the crowd and found you again. I want you to know how sorry I am for everything you told me over the years because you did not deserve any of that, especially that bullshit with Alvin. I am going to fix everything and make things right, Babe. I may not have been around to protect you back then, but I am here now and will be for the rest of our life together. I am yours. I want you to enjoy yourself tomorrow and please, Babe drive carefully. We did not have enough time together and I did not want to waste what we had talking about others, but I meant to tell you to not instigate that bitch. See, she only wants me when she sees someone else does. She has ruined two other relationships of mine because they let her lies get the best of them. I love how you took the initiative and did your investigation, but please don't put yourself in a position for her to ruin us. I cannot live without you, Pumpkin, and I would seriously hurt that bitch over you. Anyway, my Love, I still can't believe I saw you today, I have waited 14 years for those moments we shared this morning, it was all I ever dreamed it would and more. Your smile is so pretty up close and personal, and I appreciate you being defensive about your husband and our relationship, Baby. Well it took me almost seven hours to finally stop shaking so I'm gone spend the rest of tonight thinking about you, Beautiful. I'll be playing memories of our time together over and over until I fall asleep. I am pausing this special moment in time and absolutely so deep in love with you, Shanna. Princess, I love you so much and I thank you for going through what you had to in order to visit me, Love. Have a good night, Sweetheart. Be careful and make sure you tell my Taylen I love him. Our journey had officially begun, Babe, nothing can compare to what I am feeling.

Love Always Mr. Herring

I love you, I love you, I love you, I love you, Shanna

8-25-2014
Song: Chante Moore I'm Keeping You

Baby Girl,

Sweetheart I thought about you today as I do every day, reflecting on our time together which seems like a distant memory and one I will cherish forever. Shanna, I fell in love with you all over again. You have me on such a high. I can't explain the mornings with us waking up next to one another are not so far and I don't believe I can be any closer to heaven than where we are. I miss the way you smell, Baby. I miss the way it feels to have your pretty little hands entangled in mine. I hope you and Tay had fun at Sesame Place and I apologize for not being able to be there, but we will have our family time soon, my Love. I know you are going to smile when you get back home to find a pile of mail from me. I love your smile, Baby, you wear it well. I forgot to mention that I hope you aren't bothered by me saying I'm seeing your birthmark on your tongue. I think it's one of many things that make my Princess unique and I hope you let me taste it. I still cannot get over the reality that my wife really sat in front of me. I wish we had more time, Babe, because it crushed me to let you go like that. I know I have a few things I may need to work on, but I hope you liked what you saw, and I hope you felt safe. Sweetheart, I have dreamed and anticipated that moment for over ten years and I couldn't have experienced anything better. You literally took my breath away the very moment our eyes met, Babe, you really are so beautiful inside and out. Anyway, Sexy, today is Monday and I still ain't get the second book you sent so if it doesn't come tomorrow, I will have mom let you know. I'm hoping it was out of stock and they refunded your money cause if not, it's gone be problems. It was turning me on when you started buggin when I told you I hadn't received it. I was like damn my baby about to curse somebody out over her husband. On another note, Sweetheart, I will never be able to put into words how deeply touched that you came to me. I really appreciate it, Boo. I hope you drive safely on your way out of Jersey because I will lose it if anything goes otherwise. I am anxious to know what your mom's opinion of everything once you tell her about our visit. Okay Beautiful, I did not want to make this particular letter too long. I just needed to express what was in my heart which is you and belongs to you. I can't wait to hear your voice again, Pumpkin, because I really miss you. So, let me go for now, but I will be writing you again soon, Babe. You know you are all I think about, no seriously. I am excited about our journey together and us furnishing our home together. I can't wait to be with you. Shanna, I love you with all of my heart, Baby Girl, and will speak to you soon. Kiss my little one for me and please be careful down there, Baby. I'll be home soon. I love you Mrs. Herring and I will never love another.

 Love Eternally, Lance

I'll never forget the way I felt when I first laid eyes on you. You are the one, Baby, you were always the only one.

8-27-2014
Song: Alex Bugnon Missing You

Mrs. Herring,

How are you doing beautiful? I hope you made it back to
North Carolina safely from here and to your grandma's
house by the time this letter reaches you. It really pissed
me off earlier to hear how aggravated you were because
of that bullshit Alvin pulled. I was expecting you to be
happy after seeing me and spending time with Taylen at
Sesame Place, but unfortunately things didn't go that way.
Okay, let me change the subject because that shit is about
to piss me off all over again. I don't know what your
brother's waiting on cause they should've been lit his ass
up, but I really hope shit works out before I get home
because I'm not dealing with that shit and I ain't doing no
talking. Anyway, Sweetheart it has been driving me crazy
on the low that now since I know exactly how it feels to
touch you, it makes it that much harder to be away from
you. Babe let me just remind you that anything that
involves you and my son being mishandled or mistreated,
I take that shit extremely personal. On the same hand
though, I am here for you Babe, you always have my
support. So I don't want you to be feeling like you are
overwhelmed because you don't have nothing. You have
me. Hopefully, the reality of our relationship along with

the direction we are headed in together is setting in more since we actually spent a little time together. I know for me the loving feelings I have always had for you have intensified, like my passion runs deep for you my Love. Being with you is still a dream to me and I am just ready to come home and be with our family. You don't know how bad I wanted to keep kissing your neck, but I ain't wanna give you the wrong impression, you know. It's just that I have 14 years of love and affection that I am anxiously waiting to give you, but I swear, Baby Girl, forever isn't enough time for what I have in mind for you. Okay, Baby, I just wanted to write you a short note to welcome you home and tell you how much I miss you already. I believe the number should be approved sometime this week, so hopefully I'll be able to call my Baby and hear your voice. Shanna, I love you, Babe, and I want you to be careful down there, oka? Have a good morning my love, I will be speaking to you again soon. Give the little one a kiss from me. I love you, Mrs. Herring.

Love Always, Mr. Herring

8-31-2014

Song: Switch I Call Your Name

Mrs. Herring,

Hey Love, I hope this reaches you with a smile and at home safely after your busy week traveling. I got so used to writing you every day and now that because I haven't in a few days, it feels like mad long since I sent you something. Baby, being able to speak to you on the phone for the short 2- hours we had, reminded me of older times and I was loving every minute, Babe. I could not keep you off my mind at all, so if you didn't get much sleep, my bad. Shanna I woke up this morning and saw the sunrise a little differently than I usually do because I watched it with you in my heart. Even the way I miss you now feels different than before, Baby, and you don't know how bad I want to be home with you. I don't know how you did this to me, Pumpkin, or what magic you possess that has kept me so in love with you for all these years. I know you gone laugh, but Little Mama, you don't understand, listening to your voice is like music for my soul, and even writing your name, Sweetheart, has an addictive lust. We spoke on a few different topics yesterday, but I hope things sunk in when I was telling you how much I love you and our little one, and how with you is the only place my heart belongs. One more thing, Babe, I did feel some kind of way about you saying you did not want any more children, and the only reason you would give me one is because I don't have any. I don't know how sure you are, but I do believe that stupid ass ruined your whole experience of how motherhood is supposed to be. I'm not going to dwell on this, but it does bother me a little because I want my children with you. Anyway, though I'm sure it's still hot down there today cause it is hot as hell up here. But I need you to start drinking more water. You also need to start eating like you supposed to, especially breakfast, my Love, even though you are not big on breakfast. Can you believe I am laying here writing you and watching Cars movie, I think this is Part 2? I was like damn, I could be in our living room sitting on the floor with Taylen watching this, lol and making sure he don't wipe the grease from his popcorn on the couch because you gone trip. Oh yeah, Ms. Lady, I ain't forget how you tried to play me like a weirdo because I wanted you to take a picture of your pedicure. Boo, you ain't realize yet that I love every part of you, every curve, every single hair, and I do intend to show you exactly how much I love you really soon. Well, Beautiful, I'm gone finish laying here thinking about my everything and staring at this picture I have of you. I know I've been sending you a lot of mail and since you have a lot going on. I do not expect a response to all of them. The phone list should be approved by the time you get this letter, so expect a call from me, Babe. We ran that $50 down to like $18 yesterday, so I got to put more on the line so I can talk to my Queen. I love you though, Shanna, and I miss you even more, Sweetheart. Give Taylen a kiss for me, I want him to always know how important he is to me. Mrs. Herring, I love you with all my heart Baby Girl, speak to you soon.

Love Mr. Herring

I'm looking forward to our first meal together as a family, and I want my dessert to be you. Don't forget to send me that list of jobs Baby. I love you and appreciate how you take care of me, Love.

9-2-2014

Song: Freddie Jackson Love is Just A Cloud Away

Baby Girl,

Hello Beautiful, I finally got the letter you wrote to me on your first day home after making that long-ass drive to see me. Thank you again, Sweetheart. Trust and believe that I am missing my Queen just as badly now that you are back home. Babe, I don't want to ever kiss another female, look into anyone else's eyes, or hold another woman's hand except yours, Boo. I still can't stop thinking about that kiss. Damn Baby, your lips are so soft and they taste so sweet and I wish you would've tongued me down. Shit it would have been way more difficult for me to hide my dick being hard than it would have been for you once your juice started to flow. Babe I'm glad to hear that you feel safe with me and in my arms because I want to keep you in those places forever. You just fit in my embrace so perfectly Baby, and just the thought of your sexy ass pressed against my body is about to drive me crazy. The time is almost near when you will see me every day, Love, before you go to sleep and when you open your pretty brown eyes in the morning. While I am on the topic of how special you are, I also want you to know how much I appreciate all of the inconvenience you endured to send me books and stuff, Babe. On another note, Pumpkin, hopefully by now, you got my little drawing of how I want our venue staged as far as the seating goes. I have been beyond ready for you to be my wife before God and share my last name, my Love. I also meant exactly what I said about my little one and him having our family name. Baby, that wasn't just talk because in my heart, he is mine anyway. I miss you so much, Shanna. You just don't know, Babe! You also don't know that when you were sitting in front of me, I kept thinking about variety of ways to put hickeys on your inner thigh and along your collar bone. You was just sitting there thick in all the right places looking so fucking good, Babe. You made me feel like a kid in a candy store. I just wanted to taste everything at once. I don't want you to change anything sweetheart, how can you change something already so perfect? Yeah, Babe, I been made shit clear to my ex and that chapter in my life is closed, I would never leave you for anyone nor would I do anything to mess up this beautiful life that we are building. I love you too much, Shanna. How your mom's gonna tell you she hoped you wore something cute when you came to see me? Don't she know my love for you is unconditional? Babe, I love your sense of style because you are versatile. Anything my wife puts on, she makes look good and not that it matters, because I want you for the woman you are, in all your slender. Babe, I am beyond happy with everything about you and that can never change. Your only competition is yourself, them other bitches will never come close to being half of who you are. I do believe that God is keeping us on track so we can be together because as time passes, I am seeing my dreams with you come true. Let me also tell you how honored and really flattered I am to hear you think that I'm sexy. You are the only person I want to look good for, Baby, your opinion of me is all that matters. I started working out the week before you came and I'm going to stay consistent so that when I get home to you I can make your panties wet. I also have been thinking that since I haven't had sex in seven years and since you are being abstinent out of respect for our marriage, I wasn't going to masturbate anymore since you don't do that either. I mean, it is going to be hard because looking at you and thinking about you always does something to me and I be wanting you so bad, Little Mama, so we will see. After your long trip, I would have put you in the bath with a glass of champagne, while I made dinner for you once I unpacked your suitcases. Baby, I want to be there to hold you and help you relax, until you are rested enough for me to show you how much I missed my wifey while she was away. Damn Love, I don't know how I'll be able to fight it with you riding me and just looking in your eyes while we make love. I can't wait Babe. I think our love life is going to be off the hook because there is nothing I won't do to you in our bedroom and I mean nothing. I believe every time that we make love, it will be very passionate and intense. To answer your other question, my Love, when I dream about you, it is always about us spending time together, like me laying in your lap and just our life in our home, Babe. Other times, I get the ones where I am between your legs and I can see your sexy faces as we make love and that shit be feeling so real, LaShanna, like your heels be digging into my lower back making me stroke deeper inside of you. Okay, Mrs. Herring, on a serious note, about us getting a family lawyer. I am concerned about the expense, but I also believe in taking guns to knives fights. I mean Alvin is a dumb ass, so I doubt he is seeking legal counsel, but I want us to take every precaution to secure our success. Can I ask you something, Babe, am I wrong for wanting to keep Taylen to ourselves?, cause I honestly feel like he just doing this to make shit difficult. I do not believe in my heart that he loves my son, definitely not like me. I know you said she wants $300 an hour, but if she is only putting a motion in, that's not an hour of work. Whatever you decide, Baby Girl, your man supports you 100%, and if you have to borrow the money, I will send a money order once a month with what I can afford until it is paid. I also read through the brochures you sent about the wedding venue and so far I like the Renaissance Resort because our guests can stay in the hotel and we can host our wedding all in the same place. However, I do want something more original and a hotel sounds tacky, but this is a high-end resort and they will decorate to our liking. As far as the food goes, the buffet sounds nice, but Babe, we black, and you know how 'black folks get at buffets. A plated dinner seems more cost effective and plus, we can all have our appetizer, main course, and dessert at the same time. This way, the event staff can clean the floor and not have to wait for straggles. It depends though, Babe and we'll discuss this on the phone. What flavor do you have in mind for the cake, Babe? You know what I like, plus it matches our colors. But I wanna know what my Princess likes. Don't forget, I can't dance Babe. I just put some more bread on the phone so I can call you at home directly at the end of the week. I really miss you, LaShanna and anything I have ever really looked forward to in my life always seems to be centered around you. I can't wait until our wedding day Babe, but I am and always will be yours forever. Oh yea, I'm telling you now, ain't nobody getting your garter so we mind as well skip that part. You are going to be so beautiful in your dress, Babe, and I can already feel tears building as I imagine my queen and the love of my life, walking down the aisle. Well, Gorgeous, I will be pausing this moment here for now, and my Love, undying adoration grows stronger for you each day. I will trust God and patiently wait until the next time we meet. Forever, Shanna, I love you, Babe a million times and a billion times that. I will be missing you and my Taylen until I hear, see, or speak to you again. I love you sooo much, Mrs. Herring and keep smiling for me, Beautiful and kiss my son for me.

Love Forever, Your Husband, Mr. Herring

9-5-2014

Song: Aaliyah One in a Million

Baby Girl,

It's only been about twenty minutes since our last call and already I am missing you, Sweetheart. I really enjoyed our conversation and it feels good that we still have that same chemistry that we had all those years ago. The way it sounds when you are smiling always lights me up on the inside. I love you so much, Babe. I want you to remember what I said about you stressing over and not feeling like you are making progress. Sweetheart, you made me see that God has a plan for us and we are exactly where he needs us to be at this point. Shanna, you are not alone, my Love and I am here with you and things are working themselves out boo, trust me. I finally took the book you sent me out of its packaging and I can't wait to start reading it, Babe. Anything I can learn that will help me in becoming a better husband and man for my Princess, I'm with it. Don't be trippin about them donuts, Baby, enjoy yourself because I love your body. I be lusting over you so hard most of the time and you know I prefer you thick, and you really are so fucking sexy, Babe. Anyway, Love, it's like 4:05 pm so I know you are getting yourself together so you can pick our son up from school. I really hope he behaved himself because I am anxious to know how he has been acting up lately. Damn, we still haven't decided on the details of our wedding, Babe. I am willing to have the ceremony you want because we deserve it, but I am so ready for you to be my wife, Babe. You are my wife already, but you know what I mean. You should see me, Pumpkin, looking back and forth at this damn watch. I want this next two hours to hurry the fuck up so I can hear my Baby's voice again. I like how you laughed at my drawing too. No, I didn't pass art class because I was always in the principal office or cutting that class. Shit, I haven't exactly seen no Picasso or Mona Lisa from you either. See Shanna, this is another thing I adore about this love we share: the love between us is so intense, yet we still can pop shit and joke with one another. Plus you know already that seeing your beautiful smile or hearing your laugh does something to me, Babe. Seriously though, my Heart, if you are serious about renewing your Sora license, you should go ahead and start the process Boo, even if I can't pay for it in full right now. I will have half for you. LaShanna, you have added so many priceless things to my life, my Love, and you have given me a best friend. You have given me a very beautiful and devoted wife, and you gave me a baby boy. Honestly, speaking, Baby Girl, my life would have no value if not for these special things you have added to it. So don't ever feel like you are taking from me and I am going without. I know sincerely that as long as I have you and my son, I have everything I will ever need and much more. So, Sexy, having said these things, I need to pause this moment in love with you. Not for long, Baby, only long enough to start on your other letter. Mrs. Herring, it is still amazing to me the way it feels to be in love with you because you are special, Babe, and you are my everything. I would have really liked to have breathed in your sweet scent a little deeper and to gently suck on your neck longer during our visit. Yes, I would love to kiss those soft and sexy lips all over again. Okay, Little Mama let me go for now so I can start on your other letter. Baby, I truly love you so much and can't wait to call home and speak to my Princess again. I love you, Babe, and give our son a kiss for me to. And he doesn't get any Krispy Kreme until after dinner Babe, if he behaves himself. Damn girl, I love you for real for real, I'm never leaving you, Sweetheart.

Love Always, Lance, Your Husband Then, Now, and Forever

Song: Tank Sex Music

Babe,

I stop and look at you, waiting for your breathing to slow and I let you watch me suck that gooey sweetness from my fingers, I don't want you to cum yet. I then turn you over and kiss you slowly from the back of your ankles up to your calf muscles, working my way up to where your soft ass and the back of your thighs meet. I pause briefly when I notice the juices glistening on your pussy. Teasing you while the heat of my breath tickles your ass. Then I take my tongue using the tip and lick you slowly from the opening of your vagina and up the split of your ass. Stopping only to continue kissing you slowly along your spine. I leave traces of my wet kisses up your back moving only body up gradually until I reach the back of your neck. I see you biting your lip with your eyes tightly shut, as I nibble and suck along your neck and earlobes. Baby, I can feel you move your hips under me and your ass is grinding past my dick. I want you to feel how hard I am for you, I want you to feel how turned on you have me. Now I turn your body over again, continuing to suck on your neck making my way between your throat and back to your sweet lips. You are kissing me a little rougher now, so I know you want me. So I work my way to your nipples. Babe, your titties are so perfect and I am gently tugging your left nipple between my teeth and running my warm tongue over it to add pleasure to the pain. I take my time and show your right nipple equal attention. Sucking it into my mouth a little harder, while gently massaging the other with my fingertips. It is time for me to kiss my way down the center of your chest towards your navel and everywhere around your stomach. My dick is so hard, Babe, from the sight of you laying here naked. I love your curves and I love the way your soft skin tastes. Finally I reach the top of your pelvic bone and I lick the left side of your pussy. I feel you spreading your legs putting one on my back with the heel of your other foot resting on my shoulder. I have waited for what feels like an eternity to taste your sweetness. And taking my tongue, I part your pussy lips slowly. Pausing to lick the moisture from my own lips because you are so wet now, Baby. My wet tongue is moving across your vagina warm hole. I love the way your pussy taste. I then slowly use the tip to lick around your clitoris and because it is exposed now, I can wrap my lips around it, and gently holding it firmly while I massage it with my mouth. I am watching the pace of your breathing speed up and I know this feels good to you because your hand is on the back of my head keeping me in place and you are grabbing our bed sheets with your other. The sounds of your moans are making me want to fuck you so bad, I feel my dick hanging out of the opening of my boxers because I am so hard. Baby, your moans are getting longer and louder now. I am holding your waist with my hands so you don't squirm too much, but your nectar is flowing out of you and I don't want to waste any so I suck your pussy hole just to remove the excess. I know the sound of the slurp made you hornier. I continue to roll my tongue around your clitoris until you begin to say my name but stopped short because of the way your body just trembled. I know you are about to release all of the honey you have and need to release into my mouth and I suck gently on your clitoris while I lick it left and right, back and forth. Now I feel your legs begin to shake and you pull my face deeper into your pussy, Baby, it feels so good, and you sound like you want to cry. By the way you are breathing, I know you are coming to the end of your orgasm. I have waited so long to make love to you, Baby, to be inside of you and have you stare into my eyes. Now I am moving up onto the bed as I slide my boxers all the way off. I lean forward to kiss you and I am holding the base of my dick searching for your hot pussy so I can slide it in the entrance. I feel you reach down taking my dick in your little hands firmly and I feel you brush my hard tip against your wet opening. Now you look into my eyes and then you.... you have to finish the next part, Baby, I'll be waiting I love you and can't wait to make this cum true.

9-7-2014

My Dearest Love,

Good Morning, Sweetheart, I wanted to begin this letter by thanking you for the smile I woke up with and the peace in my heart. Speaking to you makes me feel so alive Babe, and as much as I want to wait until Tuesday to call home and speak to you, I probably won't make it. I use the term "Call Home" because my home is and always will be where my Queen is. It is about 9:40am right now and I've been awake since like five something, I wonder if you and my son are up yet. Baby, make sure you don't have the A.C blowing all on you because I don't want you to catch a cold, especially since I am not home yet to take care of you. Also Babe, I really appreciate you sending me that book. I like that you wanted to share that information with me so don't take what I said like I ain't like it. Actually went back a little while ago after I worked out and read through two random chapters, I am glad I did. Everything you send me has a special meaning to me and I even have some custom labels I use to put on the books you send me. For real though, Princess, I have some clarity now that I was unsure of previously, so I view the way the author said things in a whole new light. So thank you Love. Shanna, I miss you so much, Babe, it doesn't feel like I talked to you yesterday or that you were here two weeks ago. You are so addictive and you don't even know it. Boo, you keep me chasing constantly for that next fix. You make loving you so easy, Babe, and beyond worth it. Which is why it confuses me how others have had the privilege of having a goddess in their lives, and letting you slip away. I am glad things worked themselves out the way they have though because I always knew I was made to love you in ways that no one else could even understand. Sweetheart, you will never be alone again and you are far from a single mother because I have always been here. I always been yours. Pumpkin, I want you to stay on top of renewing that license, Babe, and you need to mentally prepare for your schedule to change cause I have been getting this feeling like you are going to hear from one of those companies you applied for. I want to be holding your hand, Baby, even if we are just in the living room sitting together. I would give anything to feel your touch. Hopefully, I'll be starting my new job soon which pays more so I will be able to help my wife with whatever she may need. Shit, I'll even send your mom's like $40 a month so she can leave you alone about money. Just don't let things overwhelm you, Shanna. I am on the way home, Sweetheart. And whether or not we can see it yet, God is lining things up to help us reach destination.

My mind, body, and soul are focused on being with the love of my life and nothing is going to get in the way of that I promise. Oh yea, Boo, I don't remember which questions from the book that I was suppose to answer, so I'll pick a chapter randomly until you let me know. LaShanna, OMG, Baby, I am really deeply in love with you, like you got me intoxicated and infatuate with any and everything that has to do with you, Little Mama. I hope that makes sense, to you but it is very very hard trying to explain in words, how special you are and how I feel about your sexy ass. Well, Sunshine, let me go for now so I can answer those questions. There is a fire that burns throughout my insides for you that can never be put out. I love and adore you so much, Mrs. Herring, and I can't wait to keep showing you through my actions. Drive safely, Sweetheart, and wherever you are, know your husband is thinking about you. Kiss my Taylen for me. I love you, Babe, always.

Love Eternally, Mr. Herring

9-13-2014
Song: Dave Hollister Spend the Night

Beautiful,

How are you doing my Love? I have been missing you since we last spoke and then when no letters came from you this week I started to worry about you, Babe. So it is good to finally hear from you. And you must have sent this earlier in the week, so I don't know why I'm just getting it on Saturday. Anyway, Sweetheart, my love and desire for you continue to grow stronger as well as my devotion to remain committed to this special love we share. About our wedding, I want to see you in a dress, Boo, and I want all the bells and whistles that our dream come true deserves. What I don't want is to have to be without you legally until we can afford our ceremony. LaShanna, I want us to be together and, Baby, I want to marry you…I don't want to keep waiting though due to financial limits. Hypothetically speaking, if we went to the courthouse, it would depend on where we are when we decide to be wed. I want my mother to be my witness so to have her come all the way to N.C seems unreasonable. On the other hand, I'm not sure of who your witness would be, but we really need to figure this out. Just remember, Babe, I will marry you my first day home if it were possible, and you were willing. Babe, I want you to only have my last name. I don't even like writing your maiden name on my letters, but you told me too because of the mail lady. Shanna, I really miss hearing your voice, Baby, and I can tell you don't wanna write anymore by how long it took me to get this letter. It was definitely a pleasure to be able to talk to my wife. Shit if I had more money, I would have put it on the phone already. Boo, it's good to hear you say I am your 'Proverbs 31 man', and I promise to keep living up to that.. All I have ever wanted to do was give you all of my love and now I can, to you and Tay. Speaking of my little one, I got the invoice from the company a few days ago so his books should have come by time you get this letter. I just hope he likes them and won't think dumbass sent them. Princess, don't be sad about the wedding magazines because we are still figuring things out and have not made a definite decision. On another note, I see you finished our story. Damn babe, you ain't do nothing but throw gas on the fire. Babe, you had my dick so hard, I had to sit up in the bed to hide that shit, especially, the part with you riding me. You have been on my mind so heavy, my Love, I got lonely as hell the other day out of nowhere. And it wasn't in the sense of being alone and having nobody, it was like I have a void or a missing piece of me that only you can comfort, only you can fill. So, Boo, I understand now what you mean when you say you get lonely at times and it bothers you that I am not around. Anyway, Love, despite the way I felt, everything else has been okay this week. I just can't wait for these 90 days to be over. They about to do this food package shit and I want some Sunflower Seeds and Captain Crunch. Don't laugh at me, I know I'm greedy. Okay Sexy, I am starting to ramble so let me go for now. Baby, I want you to know I stay thinking about you and I miss you so much. I look forward to our next hug and kiss. I can't live without that for too long. I love you with all of my heart Mrs. Herring, make sure you travel safe and kiss my Taylen for me. Have a goodnight, Beautiful. I am so blessed to have you in my life, Babe, I love you.

Love, Lance Forever, Your Husband

9-15-2014

Song:   Mack Wilds Don't Turn Me Down
         Chris Brown Take You Down

Baby,

I am so glad to get another letter from you, Sweetheart because I have been dealing with some bullshit for a few days now and I swear I was reaching the point where I wanted to bug out. Babe, these niggas have had the electricity and ventilation system shut off since Thursday, so even though it's 70° outside, and it's at least 89° in these cells. You know how I feel about the heat. After getting your letter though, Boo, and going through my pictures, me seeing newborn Taylen had a very special effect on me. It was like something was reminding me that I have a wife and son waiting on me, and I need to be at home with my family. I mean, just seeing both of you put me back there during that time with you in the hospital and it put me on the verge of tears, Babe. I just don't understand how I carry myself a certain way, and I am usually in a violent state of mind ready to react to whatever may happen around me. Yet somehow you always break me down like this. Loving you and Taylen sheds my armor and brings me to my knees, Babe, I love you both so much. Thank you for sending me pictures, my Love. You know I am obsessed with admiring your booty, oops beauty. LaShanna, your body looks absolutely perfect to me, I see you tried to cheat cause some of your right side isn't in the picture. You did not have to cover your stomach either, Little Mama, I love every part of your sexy ass from head to toe. I liked your polka dot panties. I will kiss every dot when I get there. I didn't know lace looked like that. Speaking of your head and toes, your hair is getting longer, Sweetheart, and your feet are perfect. I never liked feet, Babe, but yours are perfect. They are all small and pretty, I definitely have some whipped cream plans for those, watch and see. It looked like Tay had fun at Sesame Place, but where were you, Babe? You should have taken a picture or two while you were there. This is random, but Shanna, your letters, and your scent smells so fucking good, Babe. As soon as I smelled it and saw the very sexy pictures of you, it made me horny as hell, Babe. My dick is still hard and has been the entire time I've been writing you. Anyway, Pumpkin, I hope Tay liked the books and I'm sorry the UPS lady woke you from your beauty nap. I saw the smile on his face. He looks so much like you. I swear though, Babe, his baby picture looks exactly like mine. I think that's what brought the tears. No, of course, I did not forget that you like Pooh because he is also my mother's favorite, and yes I read between the lines. Did I mention to you yet how much I love you, Babe, or that I am missing my wife so much. I just wanted to make time and tell you that my, Queen. Yes Shanna, you still consume my every waking thought and I lose sleep each night from your divine visits in my dreams. Again, Baby, I love you so much, and I will always be here for you, Sweetheart. I will be here now and then should any issue arise with our custody battle. Since you decided to do the security for a while, let me know if you need half the money to renew your license Babe. I'm glad you are aware of the fast approaching holiday season and what you getting me? Lol. I like the rings you chose, but you know my pride feels like you need something better, and I'll upgrade you when I get home, my Love. I'm going to do the ring sizing thing and send it back to you, but I am still trying to clear it with the mailroom Sgt. I'll do it tomorrow, Babe. I set some money aside to put towards our rings, and also put a couple dollars on the phone so I can hear my Wifey's sexy voice. I will be answering one chapter of questions from our book and send one chapter with each letter until they are complete. This nonsense with the power got in the way of my workout, but supposedly it will be fixed tomorrow.

Shanna, I can't wait until the next time we are together again so I can wrap my angel up tightly in my arms. My body is calling for you Sweetheart. Just so you know, Babe, I fall in love with you all over again each day, and always deeper than the day before. So when you said Happy Anniversary to me, I just relive the celebration of my love and devotion to you. Hold on, Babe, I really want you to know how much I appreciate you for the way you love and support me. LaShanna, you are such a wonderful lady and there won't ever come a day where I won't be proud to say you are mine. I am so humbled every time I look at you in my mind or otherwise, because God has blessed me beyond words. I saw some talk show that Tamar is on and she said she don't let her husband be on IG or Facebook cause his are "theirs" and so another girl was like well he gotta have a life too and Tamar moves her hands over her body and says "Can't you see all the life I'm giving him. I'm all the life he needs". So initially, I thought she was on some conceited shit, but after looking at you, Baby, and meditating on how I feel about you, I get it now. You give me life, Pumpkin, and as long as I have my beautiful butterfly, I don't want or need anything else. Well, my Love, having said all of this, I feel the need to remind you that you are very special and your husband loves you eternally, Babe. Okay Sexy, let me go for now so I can start on some of those questions. But I thank you again for the pictures, Baby. Shanna you mean the world to me my Love. Have a goodnight and kiss my Taylen for me. I will call you in a few days, Love. Until then, drive safely and know you are on my mind. I love you so much.

Love Now and Forever, Mr. Herring

I'll call Friday to see how you did on your 5k run, I still want pictures too. Stay sexy and keep smiling for me, Boo.. better yet, Mrs. Herring, because I'm nasty. Damn, you keep me so turned on. I love you.

9-18-2014
Song: Barry White Never Gonna Give You Up
     Elle Varner Refill

Mrs. Herring,

When this letter reaches your pretty brown eyes, I hope you are smiling, Babe, and I pray that more than anything, this is another reminder of how much I love you, Sweetheart. If my little one is home, please call him to you baby and give him a kiss. Although he is too young to understand, I need you to tell him that I love him. Please, my Love, do that for me as soon as you are able. I have been staring at my priceless collection of photos of you and Taylen. Babe, I have been smiling deeply on the inside because you make me so happy. Whenever I look at you, all I see is sunshine. You and my son are an invaluable gift to recompensate for all of the rainy days I have had in my life. Shanna, how can I truly begin to describe to you a love that runs so deep. Baby, I am missing you like crazy and I did not want to take for granted anytime I had to share with you how important having you in my life is. I did put some money on the phone, but they still haven't activated it yet, I'm going to check again tonight because I need to hear your voice, Pumpkin. I wonder what you have been doing over the past couple of days? Wondering if my wife is okay and if you can feel me missing you so much. You probably are going to curse me out, but I still haven't measured my finger. We have no access to scissors, Babe. I'm working on it though. Unfortunately though unless we fax them our marriage certificate, they won't let you send me my ring. However, Babe, if you wore it when you came to see me again, like on your thumb, I could just slip it on my finger unnoticed. Anyway, Beautiful, Summer is officially over on Monday. One more month gone and closer to being home with my Baby Girl. How has my Taylen been doing in school and how has his behavior been at home? I am so proud of the mother you are, Sweetheart, and grateful as well, for the nurturing wife and friend you are to me. When I think about how far we have come, I love the fact that our love is the stuff love fairy tales are made from. I always prayed and asked for God to let me marry you. Yep all the way back then I wanted you forever, Shanna. And I always will, Baby. I meant to ask you, Babe, how long once you start working do you intend to look for a place and what do you have in mind? I almost forgot to mention to you, Sexy, that I was watching 'Four Weddings' the other day and this couple had an Alice and Wonderland theme. All of her decorations was red and black. I was like my wife would love this, especially the cake, Bae, it was nice. I was also watching HGTV and saw this nice resort in Myrtle Beach and we have to vacation there one day. Well, Boo,

I'm still waiting to hear from you. Maybe I'll get a letter tomorrow either way the phone should be on so I can call you. Listen, I did not intend for this to be a long letter, Baby, so I will end it here for you now, while my love never ceases. Shanna, I love you and I miss you, Princess. And I am glad God blessed me with a conscious and subconscious mind so I can think about you and live in love with you infinitely. I want you to have a good evening, Babe, and catch the kiss I am blowing you. You can put them wherever you want. Don't forget to tell the little one what I said. I shall anxiously wait to hear from you again my love. Goodnight, Mrs. Herring I love you always.

Love Forever, Mr. Herring

I would walk a million miles and one thousand days just to feel your touch, and just to let you feel me whisper in your ear that I LOVE YOU.

To Be Continue....

This Bid is Not Over

## About This Author

LaShawn McCallum was born and raised in Jersey City, NJ. She moved to Raleigh, North Carolina in 2012 to start a new journey in life. She has one child, who she adores very much. In LaShawn's spare time, she loves to write, whether poetry or starting on a good book. She loves to read and has a wide collection of books in her library.

Contact Info:
Soul Heart Publishing
P.O Box 41287
Raleigh N.C 27629

Iam_CagedHeart (Instagram)

www.ingramcontent.com/pod-product-compliance
Lightning Source LLC
Chambersburg PA
CBHW031213020726
47499CB00002B/560